Praise for Leanne Hall

'A surrealist mystery (what could be more intriguing than that?) and a fantastic journey through life, art, people and families. Wise, whimsical, delightfully original and altogether charming.' Cassandra Golds on *Iris and the Tiger*

'Reminiscent of Elizabeth Goudge's classic *The Little White Horse*, full of mystery and an enchanting sense of elsewhere.' Martine Murray on *Iris and the Tiger*

'Refreshingly original, Hall's debut novel has a genuine edge. It's *Blade Runner* meets *Peter Pan* with a bit of sweetness, sadness and tension.' *Sunday Age* on *This Is Shyness*

'For more mature readers who choose to trespass into the realm of young-adult fiction, *This Is Shyness* is just the book to revive a faded sense of rebellion and adventure.' *Weekend Australian* on *This Is Shyness*

'It's original, it's edgy, it skirts the borders of fantasy while being anchored in the real world, and it's totally absorbing. The long night is over, but we know the story continues. More please.' *Good Reading* on *This Is Shyness*

'This inventive read successfully combines elements of contemporary teen lit, dystopian adventures, and *The X-Men* into a delicate, elliptical, and heartfelt genre all its own.' *Kirkus* on *Queen of the Night*

Leanne Hall is the author of two novels for young adults, the Text Prize-winning *This Is Shyness* and its sequel, *Queen of the Night*. Leanne has worked in the arts, educational publishing and as a bookseller, but her enduring passion is for youth literature. *Iris and the Tiger* is her first novel for younger readers.

IRIS
and the
TIGER

Leanne Hall

TEXT PUBLISHING MELBOURNE AUSTRALIA

textpublishing.com.au

The Text Publishing Company
Swann House
22 William Street
Melbourne Victoria 3000
Australia

First published by The Text Publishing Company, 2016

Cover and internal illustrations © Sandra Eterović
Cover and page design by Imogen Stubbs
Typeset by J&M Typesetting

National Library of Australia Cataloguing-in-Publication entry:

Creator: Hall, Leanne Michelle, 1977- author.
Title: Iris and the tiger / by Leanne Hall.
ISBN: 9781925240795 (paperback)
ISBN: 9781922253453 (ebook)
Target Audience: For young adults.
Subjects: Animals—Fiction.
             Suspense fiction.
             Young adult fiction.
Dewey Number: A823.4

This book is printed on paper certified against the Forest Stewardship Council® Standards. Griffin Press holds FSC chain-of-custody certification SGS-COC-005088. FSC promotes environmentally responsible, socially beneficial and economically viable management of the world's forests.

This project has been assisted by the Commonwealth Government through the Australia Council, its arts funding and advisory body.

To Grant

No one had ever asked Iris to spy for them before.

She wasn't totally convinced she'd be any good at it. But Iris *also* wasn't in the habit of saying no to her parents—they paid her so little regard as it was—and when they first sat her down to outline their plan, Iris felt the unfamiliar glow of their attention.

'Aunt Ursula is very old now and we're worried someone might take advantage of her,' her mum had explained. 'When I knew her, she was always taking in strays. Sometimes she quite fell in love with them.'

'For example, who is this "Mr Garcia"?' Her dad made finger quotes in the air.

'I think it's *señor*, Dad.' Iris dared to correct him. 'I'm pretty sure they say *señor* over there, not mister.'

Iris was twelve years old and perfectly capable of filling in the blanks. Her parents were concerned that Great-Aunt Ursula might be going soft enough in the head to accidentally leave her entire estate to an unknown Spanish boyfriend. She wasn't really sure what she could do about it, but she would try. Besides, ten days in Spain would be far better than being stuck in the middle of the final school term. At least, that's what Iris kept telling herself.

So her interrogation of Señor Garcia began as soon as possible—on the drive from Barcelona Airport to Aunt Ursula's country home, in fact.

Iris was droopy after the long flight, but she was determined not to fall asleep on the job. Señor Garcia's navy suit draped over his bony shoulders, and a large cap similar to a policeman's hat hid his face. *He doesn't look like anybody's boyfriend*, thought Iris, as Señor Garcia beat time on the steering wheel with gloved hands.

'And what exactly is it you do, Señor Garcia?' she asked from the back seat, even though it was obvious that his job was to drive this shiny cream vintage car.

He did not answer. At the airport he had silently held up a sign saying '*IRIS CHEN-TAYLOR*', and waved at her a letter written by Aunt Ursula in loopy, old-fashioned cursive. In it, Ursula had apologised for her failure to meet her at the airport and introduced her 'dear and trusted friend, Señor Reynaldo Torres Garcia'.

Iris had no choice but to go with the tall stranger with

the shadowy face—even though it was only her second time overseas, and the first plane she'd caught on her own. But she'd already veered off the set of instructions that her dad had written down for her: Aunt Ursula was supposed to be at the airport *in person*.

'You don't speak English?' Iris asked, after their silence grew awkward. She felt the determination slide out of her voice. With no further conversation to come, she pressed herself to the car window.

The car soon turned off a main road onto a smaller one. Ahead was a gate: two fancy iron doors attached to two brick pillars. Señor Garcia sat up extra straight now; Iris could sense his excitement.

The car slowed to a crawl, and Señor Garcia pointed to a metal plaque.

BOSQUE DE NUBES

Iris squinted. *I wonder what that means?*

Her heart beat a little faster with the idea that she would soon see the house and her notorious great-aunt. Her mum hadn't told her much about Aunt Ursula's country estate, except that it was 'unforgettable'. But when Iris had asked for more details, her mum hadn't said anything, so maybe she had forgotten after all.

Trees crowded the edges of the road, leaving no verge.

They were different from Australian trees—tall and straight and almost black. When they passed a narrow path, Iris turned her head and caught a dim sparkle that might have been water.

They were the woods you read about in fairytales. Under the cover of leaves it was almost as dark as night. Iris could imagine woodcutters and bears and enchantments in their depths; you could get lost in them easily.

They're trees with secrets, she thought, and shivered.

Great Aunt Ursula's home was much further from the city than Iris had expected. The drive from the airport had taken three hours, and she'd already seen scorched hills, olive orchards, craggy mountains and terracotta-roofed villages.

After a few minutes the thick forest cleared, replaced by lawn and a scattering of ratty box hedges.

Señor Garcia followed the driveway in a wide arc before coming to a halt. He was a much smoother driver than Iris's dad. Even so, Iris felt pukey with nerves as Señor Garcia opened the door and she stumbled from the car.

The house was an enormous white mansion. It was two storeys high and had countless windows. Six columns held up the front entrance. There were arches everywhere and waves of plaster along the roof that looked like cake icing. It was the most magnificent house Iris had ever seen.

Iris felt like nothing more than a tiny speck compared with the grand old building and the ancient trees. There was ivy spreading along the walls that had to be older than she was—a thought that filled Iris with new fear. Back in Australia she'd been able to pretend that she might be able to pull this plan off. Now she wasn't so sure.

When Iris turned around a moment later, the car, her luggage and Señor Garcia had glided away. She was so tired it now seemed possible for whole cars to disappear into thin air.

Rushing down the marble steps was a woman dressed in a flapping shirt and a pair of old suit pants held up with a length of rope. Her black hair swung in a sharp bob around her face. She had a sparkly gaze and a spritely air.

'You made it!' She flung her arms out in welcome. 'I was filled with horror about the plane crashing—oh, the tearing metal, the screeching, the flames! But here you are, and all in one piece too!'

She hugged and kissed Iris noisily on both cheeks in the European way, before holding her at arm's length and giving her a good once-over.

This, Iris thought, *must be Aunt Ursula.*

Iris's mum had only one photo of Aunt Ursula. It had been taken on the beach during her own visit to Spain, more than thirty years ago. Her mum was fourteen, with too much eyeliner and too little bikini, and her hair had been teased up at the front. She swore it had been the fashion. Aunt Ursula had worn a floppy sunhat and sunglasses that covered everything but her lipsticked smile.

'Hello, Great Aunt Ursula,' Iris managed to squeeze out. Her aunt wasn't quite what she was expecting, although she couldn't pinpoint exactly why.

'I've not been in an aeroplane in over twenty years. Can you imagine?'

Aunt Ursula's voice bore only the slightest trace of an Australian accent. Her ears, neck and fingers were laden with more bling than Iris had ever seen—and not cheap, fake stuff. Her parents were right: her aunt was loaded.

'You must call me *Ursula*. *Great Aunt* makes me feel so old. Did you realise that you are the spitting image of your grandmother? Oh, you really are!'

Iris frowned. Her grandmother had been beautiful in her youth, as all her relatives had told her, so this was clearly an untruth. But Aunt Ursula had already moved on.

'I have prepared a very special poem for your arrival, Iris.'

Aunt Ursula turned and leapt up the stairs, posing dramatically in the doorframe. The cherub molded above the door looked down on her kindly. She threw a half-curled hand into the air.

'*Little flower! Little Iris!*' she barked, her face turned upwards.

Iris crossed her arms. At home, in Australia, no one ever wasted an opportunity to tell her how small she was for her age. Even on the plane, all the adults had smiled at her, as though she was terribly cute for travelling on her own.

Cute was the worst.

Little flower, little Iris
Bold clothes of brilliant purple
Liquid lavender
What do you wear at your heart, quiet flower?
Pulsing! Beating! Furious Yellow!

Aunt Ursula actually thumped herself in the heart with a fist on the final line. Iris forced herself to clap as her aunt's wails died. Aunt Ursula bowed, then curtsied, then bowed again.

Iris tried to push down her rising panic.

It's going to be a strange week.

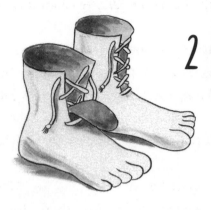

2

Aunt Ursula took Iris around the rear of the building to a marble patio hemmed by fancy railing. There were deckchairs and an umbrella, and a number of delicate wrought-iron chairs and tables.

From this height, Iris gazed over the sloping grounds of the estate. The gardens rolled away from the house as far as she could see. There were hedges and old oak trees and low stone walls. The gardens were quite overgrown, but still beautiful.

'My kingdom, if you will!' Aunt Ursula pointed theatrically. '*Bosque de Nubes* runs that-a-way, from the highway to the hills.' She sighed. 'But look at that blasted golf course! Only fifty metres from my lovely woods. Every time I see those fatheads in their checked pants and silly caps, I want to throw their clubs in the lake. So, there it is, Iris,' she said, bright again. 'The grand estate that everyone is trying to get their filthy hands on. They're all waiting for me to die, you know.'

Iris didn't know what to say. She desperately wanted to know who Aunt Ursula meant by *they*, but her father had warned that she should not, under any circumstances, talk about inheritance.

'*Bosk…de Noob*,' she blurted out. 'What does that mean in English?'

'*Bosque de Nubes*,' Aunt Ursula corrected her. 'The English translation is *Forest of Clouds*. You saw the forest on your way in? It goes for miles. A tangle of thorns and ferns, ditches and watchful trees. Rotting leaves, a swamp or two. It's a lovely place to go rambling.'

Aunt Ursula smiled down at Iris. But Iris remembered how dark and close the forest had looked from the car— anything but lovely. She tried to imagine exploring it alone and a shivery feeling ran through her again.

'The trees look like big storm clouds,' she murmured.

'Indeed,' said Aunt Ursula. 'A poetic image, Iris, but that's not where the name comes from. Several times a year a thick mist forms in the valley and hangs low in the trees for days. The trees look wonderful wrapped in puffs of white mist. The locals have parties in the woods when it happens. Though children have been known to wander off into the mists on those nights and forget themselves entirely…'

Aunt Ursula was distracted by a man in overalls and a cap who had just wandered around the corner of a nearby building. She waved.

'*Bosque de Nubes* is a large place, an exciting place,' she continued. 'You can ask me anything you want, anything you are curious about… Are you a curious person?'

Iris had plenty of questions. About the lost children and, of course, plenty of questions belonging to her dad.

'Is there a map of *Bosq*—um, the *Forest of Clouds*?' She tried to keep her voice light. 'We learnt to draw maps in Geography last term.'

Her dad's actual question included details about *infrastructure* and something called *easements*, but there was no way Iris could slip those kinds of complicated words into the conversation without giving herself away.

'And the children that go walking into the forest, in the mist,' she added belatedly, for herself, 'they come back, right? They don't get lost forever, do they?'

Aunt Ursula made a kooky clicking noise with her tongue, almost as if she disapproved.

'I wonder if you are going to be different from your mother,' she said. 'Early signs are not promising.'

A cool breeze rose up around them and rattled the leaves on the orange trees. Iris realised what it was that was unexpected about her great-aunt: she was so intense. An almost visible aura of energy crackled around her. Iris's mum had said Aunt Ursula would be well into her nineties now, but

Iris found that hard to believe.

She seems so much younger than that, she thought. *Could Mum have got it wrong?*

Inside, the house was just as impressive.

The lobby had a wide staircase that rose up like a cobra and curled around to make a balcony. There was an enormous chandelier above the main waterfall of stairs and the floor was an expanse of thousands of coloured tiles. The walls were dotted with gilt-framed portraits of people wearing fashions from hundreds of years ago.

Iris tried not to let her mouth hang open. *It just keeps getting crazier,* she thought. She craned her head, trying to figure out the size of the upper floor.

'Who else lives here?'

She knew that James, Aunt Ursula's brother, had lived here once, but he'd died years ago.

'Let's see...there's me, of course,' said Aunt Ursula. 'The gentleman outside, that's Marcel, the groundskeeper. He has a son your age. There's Señor Reynaldo Torres Garcia, who you've already met. And Elna, the housemaid. She's quite new, that one. Not entirely sure about her yet.'

'Is that all?'

Iris tried not to sound surprised. Her mum had told her about all sorts of maids and cooks and butlers from her visit.

Aunt Ursula didn't respond. She pointed left and right

like a policeman directing traffic.

'Over there is the dining room and the parlour and the main library. Through that archway are the kitchen and the laundry. That whole rear corner is where the maid lives, and Reynaldo has living quarters there too. Marcel and his son live in the cottage...'

Aunt Ursula trailed off, looking across the lobby in a distracted manner. She shuffled first in one direction, then the other, sleepwalker-style.

'The upstairs guestroom is a little poky, but I thought you'd like to stay in the same room your mother did when she was here...'

Iris watched as Aunt Ursula mumbled and drifted away, until she'd disappeared through an archway at the far end of the lobby.

Is she coming back, or is that it?

Iris stood, forgotten, in the grand space. Her ears hadn't popped since the plane, and all of a sudden she felt very, very tired. She was thousands of miles away from home, tasked with something that, it was clear to her now, was impossible. Her surrounds went in and out of focus.

'No complaints, no complaints,' she chanted under her breath.

At home, complaints were looked down on, so she'd taught herself to say these words in times of need. She was incredibly jet-lagged. Her mum *had* warned her that Aunt Ursula was unusual—and exactly the kind of person who would wander off in the middle of a conversation.

Iris took a deep breath. There was nothing to do but start up the red and gold carpeted stairs and search for the guestroom. The enormous mansion would not intimidate her.

But when she grabbed onto the banister, she felt a slither, and then a tickle on her palm. Something whipped itself around her wrist and pulled tight.

Iris drew her hand away. The banister was made of dark-red wood and had carvings of twisting vines and leaves. Iris paused until her breath returned. It was just an ordinary banister. She waited a few more seconds, and yes, that's all it was. But she still climbed the stairs with a racing heart.

The top floor had a stained-glass window and was as dim and hushed as a church.

Iris spied her suitcase and backpack on the other side of the balcony, neatly placed outside a door.

That must be my room.

The guestroom was far from poky: it was at least four times as big as her bedroom at home. It had white walls and a curved ceiling, a fat armchair in the corner, a set of drawers, a round coffee table with a vase of flowers in the middle, and a door leading to a small bathroom.

Iris dragged her luggage in. Her boring grey suitcase bore the logo of her dad's firm—Chen Architects. She'd secretly hoped for her own luggage, a purple suitcase on wheels to match her backpack, but this was all she'd been given.

Iris knelt on the enormous bed and looked out the window to the same view from the back patio, only from an even higher vantage point. From here she saw a patchwork of mottled greens. An eagle wheeled high above the garden, and there were hazy mountains in the distance. No roads, no cars, no people, no skyscrapers, trams or shops.

Iris reclined on the bed and remembered the last conversation she'd had with her parents before leaving for Spain. It had been confusing, to say the least.

'Now, we all know I had absolutely no luck getting along with that nut—with the *delightfully different* Ursula,' Iris's mum had said, smiling tensely. 'But you are much cuter than I was, Iris. Aunt Ursula must like you so much that she puts you first in her will. Spend every moment you can with her. Never disagree. Pretend you like all the things she likes. You should concentrate all your efforts on making yourself into the person you think she wants you to be.'

Iris wasn't sure she agreed with her mum's approach. *Shouldn't people be liked for who they are, not who they pretend to be?*

It soon become clear that her dad also disagreed, although for different reasons.

'The best use of your time,' he said, 'would be on information-gathering: finding out who *else* might be in your great-aunt's favour.'

Iris's mum had glared at him. Iris decided it might be a good moment to open her notebook and share her own ideas about information-gathering.

'Who does Aunt Ursula get along with best?' Iris read from her brainstorming list. 'Who does she talk to the most? Who makes her laugh, and who does she tell her secrets to? Who doesn't have much money and wants more? Who has a lot and still wants more?'

Iris glanced up. Her dad's mouth had fallen open. He was impressed, as he should be. It had taken her all morning to draw up this list. She continued.

'Who spends the most time at the house? Who uses the garden? Who owns the houses nearby and how long have they been there?'

Iris finished off with the statement of which she was most proud.

'The most important tool of a good spy is very simple— it's the eyes,' she said. 'So I will pack both my eyes, and a pair of binoculars as well.'

This was a little joke, which her parents clearly did not understand. Their expressions hadn't changed at all. Eventually her dad spoke.

'That was very good, Iris, but I need to correct you on a few points. I wouldn't bother with the neighbours. The answers will be inside the house. Also, we're not asking you to *spy*.'

'Not exactly,' added her mum.

'Spying sounds as if we have something to hide.' Her father stroked his chin with a worried look. 'We only have Aunt Ursula's best interests at heart.'

'We don't want someone else to slink in at the last minute and grab the lot,' her mum said. 'Someone with no taste, and no sense of history.'

'Imagine if they tore everything down and put in a tacky resort.'

Iris's dad thought all buildings designed by anyone other than himself were tacky. He was also obsessed with inheritances, which was understandable after he'd been frozen out of his own family's will.

Iris knew their reasoning well. 'It would be a dishonour to the friendship between Nanna and Aunt Ursula,' she said in a robot voice. No one ever noticed how good her robot voice was—it was seriously good.

'Exactly!' cried her mum. 'Win her heart, inherit the lot.'

Her dad finished up. 'And we'll be the perfect guardians until you come of age.'

3

After she'd showered and unpacked, Iris set out from the guestroom with her spy notebook tucked into her pocket. She had no plan about where she should go, and her stomach was hollow with hunger—what time was it? Her last meal had been hours ago, on the plane.

To the left of the guestroom was an unlit corridor blocked off by gold posts and velvet rope, as if people might sometimes queue there to watch a movie. Iris pushed against the rope and tried to see what was down the hallway, but it was too dark.

Imagine having a home so big you can forget about whole bits of it, she thought.

She leant over the balcony to get a better look at the paintings hanging in the more out-of-reach places. She could already see why her parents wanted to preserve Aunt Ursula's house and the gardens and one day turn the whole place into a museum. It looked like a museum already.

Ursula's brother, James Freer, had been a famous painter, so there would be lots of interest. Uncle James was the one who'd first come to Spain, after the war, and bought *Bosque de Nubes*. His paintings were worth millions of dollars, especially now he was dead.

Iris felt the faintest stir of excitement, right down deep at the pit of her stomach. It *was* cool to be in Spain, no matter how daunting and unfamiliar it was. And maybe the house would be interesting to explore, despite the impossibility of the task her parents had set her.

The paintings hanging around the lobby walls were all ordinary portraits. *Probably not painted by Uncle James*, Iris noted. Her mum had told her that she'd recognise Uncle James's paintings because they would be 'weird'. These weren't weird at all.

Somewhere on the same floor, a piano started up a cascade of rolling notes. Whoever was playing knew what they were doing. Iris forgot her stomach and the paintings, and went to investigate.

An open door on the far side of the balcony spilled out light and noise. Iris squeezed past a cleaning cart loaded with spray bottles and sponges.

The door led to a crimson room, full of couches and armchairs, tables and lamps, statues and glass-fronted cabinets. More paintings and photos decorated the walls, and another chandelier hung from the ceiling.

If this was the lounge room, it was pretty spectacular. Iris had always wondered why her mum complained about their home, but maybe she'd been comparing it to *Bosque de Nubes*.

The piano was the big, glossy concert sort with a propped-up lid. A young woman was bent so far over its keys she appeared to have no head. Sheets of music were spread out in front of her—and there were black specks swarming all over the cream paper.

Iris took two steps forward, her mouth agape. *What, what, what?* The music notes were moving!

As she got closer, Iris saw that they weren't notes at all but ants almost as big as her hand. Six of them, seven, eight—no, more than that, *dozens*. Iris closed her eyes.

This isn't happening, she told herself. *It* can't *be happening*.

When she opened her eyes again, the ants had turned back into ordinary notes.

The young woman stopped playing and swivelled to face Iris. She was wearing figure-hugging gym gear and had her hair pulled into a high ponytail. She didn't seem to have noticed the ants, even though they had almost crawled all over her hands and fingers.

'You must not tell Señorita Freer about this,' she said in heavily accented English. She closed the piano lid and stood up. 'She is jealous of me, as I am young and pretty and play piano better than her.'

The pretty part was true. The woman was around nineteen and gorgeous.

Maybe she's a model, or a dancer. Iris shook the thought off. There were more important things than Aunt Ursula's jealousy at hand.

'Where did the ants go?' she said.

The young woman blinked, then smiled disarmingly. But Iris would not be put off.

'I know what I saw,' she insisted. Then she remembered the jet lag. *Could it be making me see things that aren't really there?*

'I am Elna. You must be the Australian.'

Elna stepped behind a couch and pulled out a vacuum cleaner.

She's the maid, Iris realised with surprise. She'd been expecting someone older, not a girl in leopard-print tights and gold sneakers.

'What is your name again, little Australian?'

When she told her, Elna's mascara-coated eyes grew big. 'Iris? Same as the old man's wife.'

She dropped the vacuum hose and beckoned. Iris followed her, even though she suspected she was being distracted from the piano ants.

Together they looked at a large painting above one of the fireplaces. It showed a woman with wavy blonde hair and freckles standing in a paddock with a fawn greyhound by her side.

'Did Uncle James paint this?'

'*Sí*. You are named after his wife, Señora Iris Freer. I never met them, of course. They are dead many years.'

Elna wore hot-pink lipstick and may or may not have drawn a beauty spot above her lip.

'You have same name as dead woman.'

'Cool?' said Iris, unsure about whether this was good or creepy. Her parents had never said anything about being named after Uncle James's wife, but she supposed it could be true.

Iris Freer wore a woollen cape and khaki pants and a beret. She shielded her face from the bright sun with one hand. Long, dark shadows slanted away from her and the greyhound.

'She was a war hero,' said Elna. 'A nurse during the civil war. Very brave, at only seventeen. People still talk about her. This is not the only painting about her. The other painting is much better, actually very famous. The one with the tiger. You know this?'

'What other painting?' Iris said, distracted. She'd noticed something unusual about Iris Freer's dog and stood on tiptoes to see better. The dog had—wait, yes—the dog had *five* legs.

A sort of gentle thrill took hold of Iris, imagining some of Iris Freer's mystique could rub off on her by sharing a name. It was, of course, very unlikely that she would grow up to be someone interesting enough to paint.

Iris only realised that Elna was no longer standing beside her when she heard the vacuum cleaner start in another part of the room. Elna, like Señor Garcia the chauffeur, could move as quietly as a cat.

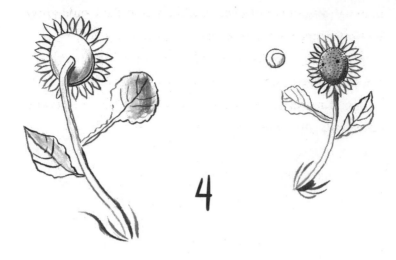

4

It was with a sense of relief that Iris stepped out of the front door and into the day. The house was creeping her out. It was so gloomy in there, and she was already struggling to stay awake.

At the side of the house was a falling-down gate, a tangle of vines and a birdbath popular with sparrows. The sun warmed the back of Iris's neck, but it was softer than the Australian sun. She squinted up. It was just after noon, maybe. In Australia, with the time difference, it would almost be her bedtime.

How will I stay awake all day?

The garden appeared normal, but Iris still felt rattled. She couldn't shake the feeling that there was something deeply strange about *Bosque de Nubes.*

She followed a raggedy brick path through a patch of tomato plants, holding out her hand when she saw a butterfly. It landed on her finger, before fluttering away at the sound of a man's voice.

Iris ducked back into the tomatoes. The voice was nearby—and getting closer. The man was speaking Spanish and he sounded angry. A leaf tickled Iris's nose but she didn't move. Two legs stopped a few metres off.

Iris peered through the vines. The man was a giant with a mobile phone—it was Marcel, she realised, who had waved at Aunt Ursula earlier. Words were spewing from him: fast, roaring words.

Marcel's face was almost completely taken up with a beard and eyebrows, and he looked as if he could rip trees out of the ground with his bare fists. Iris felt sorry for the person on the other end of the line.

When he turned away from her, Iris took the opportunity to reverse out of the veggie patch on hands and knees.

Not wanting to meet anyone else new, Iris parked herself up a tree, using a wooden crate to reach the first foothold. She settled with her back against the trunk, one leg dangling down, and pulled out her notebook.

On the inside cover she'd glued a photo of herself and her best friend Violet, taken on their first day of high school. Iris gazed at the photo, frowning. She was blinking, while Violet had a dazzling smile, thanks to two years of braces. Violet had always been pretty (they'd known each other since kindergarten), but Iris had realised recently that pretty counted for a lot in high school. And Violet always managed to keep her eyes open in photos.

Iris turned a fresh page. She went to write the date, but couldn't remember what day it was, with all the time zones and flying.

Potential toy boy, she wrote. *Marcel...mad at someone—accomplice?*

Iris capped her pen and sighed. She couldn't remember if Aunt Ursula had said what Marcel's job was at *Bosque de Nubes*. Her head was full of strangeness: the banister, the five-legged dog, the yelling, the poems. Everything in Spain was turning out to be so much harder than she'd expected it to be, and her parents should have warned her that jet lag could make you hallucinate.

Iris let her head fall against the tree and closed her eyes.

The memory of ants marched across her eyelids. From the moment she'd arrived, she'd sensed something not quite right with the estate.

She was so deep in thought that she shrieked when someone tugged on her ankle and came close to falling from the tree.

'Hello?' said a voice.

'You nearly killed me!' Iris's heart thumped sickeningly. 'No, you kill me!'

A boy stood at the foot of the tree, holding her

notebook. He acted out getting hit in the head with it.

Iris was unmoved. 'You can't go about grabbing people!'

The boy was very tanned and wore his hair long, almost to his shoulders. He looked about the same age as Iris, but none of the boys at her school would dare wear their hair like that.

'My name is Jordi and I am very pleased to meet you.'

He held out his hand. Iris leant down to shake it grudgingly.

'Iris.'

Jordi's hand felt clammy and his fingernails were dirty. *What kind of kid shook hands? Maybe it was a Spanish thing.*

'You meet my father? His name is Marcel.'

Even though Iris preferred the tree, it felt rude bellowing at Jordi from up there. She slid down the trunk and grabbed her notebook back, hoping he hadn't read any of it.

'Have you met my friends?'

Jordi pointed at a nearby shed. Two horses peered over the gate, one light brown and one dark.

'His names are Turrón and Miró.'

'*Their* names,' corrected Iris under her breath. The dark horse rolled his eyes and snorted. Iris could already tell that he didn't like her.

Jordi pulled something out of his shirt pocket and handed it to her.

'Miss Ursula ask me to give.'

It was a cream card, embossed with gold letters that said 'You are cordially invited to—' Ursula had written in elaborate calligraphy underneath:

A Surreal Dinner Party
The Ground Floor Dining Room, 8 o'clock.
Dress As Your Dreams.

'What's this?'

Iris had no idea what the word 'Surreal' meant.

Jordi shrugged, plunged his hands in his pockets. 'There is never a reason at *Bosque de Nubes*.' He smiled then, which seemed to multiply his freckles. 'Your aunt has a party if the weather is good.'

Iris found it hard not to smile. She'd forgiven Jordi for startling her. 'Are you coming to dinner too?'

'I would not miss it *for all of the worlds*.'

Jordi kept standing there and smiling, as if he expected more from her. Eventually he said, 'I know a lot about this place. Maybe you need someone who can lead you around?'

'Maybe,' said Iris. She knew the grounds were big, but surely she couldn't be a spy with Jordi in tow? He might report back to Aunt Ursula if she asked too many curious questions.

'It is a deal, okay?' Jordi shook her hand again, and Iris had the uncomfortable feeling that she'd just made an unbreakable agreement.

'I must go back to school now. Lunch is nearly closed. It was very nice meeting you.'

Jordi picked up a bike that was lying on the ground. His schoolbag was lashed to the rear rack with an octopus strap.

'Wait! Can you tell me, how far away is the town?'

Jordi made a face. 'Town? You can call it a village. Sant Joan is fifteen minutes this way. There is not much excitement there.'

Iris wasn't hoping for excitement, just an internet café. She should probably wait a few days before asking to be driven to town, in case she offended Aunt Ursula. Asking to be taken out was the same thing as saying *Bosque de Nubes* was boring.

'Oh. Well...thanks then.'

'How do you think my English is, Iris?' Jordi swung his leg over the bike. 'I try to use new sentences, but I think my accent is not so good.'

'No, it's great. Your English is three thousand per cent better than my Spanish.'

Jordi smiled and pedalled off. Iris watched him joggle across the lawns. The horses turned their heads as well. Jordi was likeable, that much was obvious.

Maybe he's *Aunt Ursula's favourite*, Iris thought. *Just my luck I'll have to make an enemy of the nicest person here.* Still, the friendly conversation with Jordi had made her feel normal again.

She read the invitation again. 'Dress As Your Dreams'—

what could that possibly mean? No one had told her she should bring clothes for a party.

Iris tucked the fancy card inside her notebook and shoved the notebook into her pocket.

When she turned back, she saw a pair of battered leather boots lined up at the base of the tree. They hadn't been there a minute ago, and she would have noticed if Jordi had left them.

The tops of the boots were regular brown leather, with laces all the way to the ankle. But then, below the ankle, the boots became…strange. The leather blended into pink skin and toes: the boots became *feet*.

Iris knelt for a closer look. It had to be a trick. The feet parts of the boots were so realistic they even had toes and toenails. Whoever made them had done a really good job.

She reached out. The toes twitched. *Like they were alive.* She jumped away with a bouncing heart.

When she dared, Iris crept up to the boots again. The leather was soft and old and wrinkled. Compared with the shimmery wonder of the ants, and the passing oddness of the leafy banister, the boots were solid and most definitely there. Their tongues hung open; some of the toenails bore traces of nail polish.

An idea slipped into Iris's mind. *They might be comfortable. Maybe they even wanted to be worn.*

Iris kicked off her sneakers and slipped her left foot into a boot. It was warm and snug. Her toes lined up neatly inside the boot's toes. Iris put on the other boot and tied the laces.

She walked up and down. The leather felt like it had merged with her skin, as if she wasn't wearing anything on her feet at all. It was the most pleasing feeling in the world.

'Where will we go?'

Iris remembered the vast gardens viewed from the guestroom window and wandered further from the house with choppy strides. It was so easy to take big steps in the boots.

Almost as if they're doing the walking for me, thought Iris.

When she glanced back, she saw Aunt Ursula in the kitchen window, working at a bench. Iris tried to reverse direction, but the feet-boots wouldn't cooperate. A chill ran through her.

The boots marched her down the grassy garden slope. Perhaps Iris was reading too much into it, but the boots seemed bossy. The sun was high and bright in the sky. Iris's forehead grew damp. She grabbed at a low-hanging branch to stop herself moving forward but couldn't keep a grip. The branch whipped back into place.

A towering hedge wall loomed. Iris's thighs already ached from trying to change direction, so she adopted a new theory: give in to the boots.

They took her around the hedge and into an enclosed garden. The garden was beautiful but neglected. Past a fountain and a sundial and straggly rose bushes lining the gravel paths.

At the centre of the garden was a statue of a nude woman who pointed up at the sky.

The feet-boots moved relentlessly towards an arch cut into the far hedge. Iris cricked her neck turning to look at the statue on the tall pedestal. From this angle Iris saw horns curling from a spot behind her ears. *Creepy.*

The statue's finger had moved to point in the direction they were travelling. Iris blinked. Sunrays sparkled across her vision and she felt tingly all over. She began to feel quite, quite strange—and not in a fun way.

She passed under the arch and into a field with waist-high grass. The sky was a piercing blue. The jagged line of forest was much closer now.

'I don't want to go in there,' she said out loud, in case the feet-boots could hear.

If they could, they didn't listen.

She was taken right to the edge of the forest. Even seeing how ordinary it all was—black trunks, tangled branches, ferny undergrowth—didn't make Iris feel any better. A trickle of sweat made its way down her spine. It was all too clear now that it had been a big mistake to put the boots on.

They followed a dirt path leading to a wire fence. When Iris realised that the fence made an enclosure, she dug her heels in. It made no difference. The feet-boots took her through a door and into the wire cage.

Dandelions and weeds pushed through the green lawn. Ghostly white lines still marked the boundaries. Across the middle was a net that sagged to the ground. The umpire's high chair was equally bedraggled. Iris was standing on a tennis court.

She took a few steps forward and realised that the feet-boots were no longer walking for her. Behind her, something cut through the air with a whoosh, followed by the definite *thwack* of a tennis ball hitting racket strings.

Iris whirled to stare at the empty court, then crouched, expecting to feel the sting of a ball thumping into her at any second.

It never happened. Another *thwack* at the opposite end of the court. Iris lifted her head and stood up.

A sunflower sprouted in the end zone. It was tall, taller than Iris. The flower raised a paddle-shaped leaf and a scrap of yellow flew above Iris's head. It reached the other end of the court, where another even bigger sunflower was waiting with two leaves raised, its yellow head bobbing.

Iris stumbled to the sidelines.

'Okay, okay, okay!' she whispered to herself.

Giant flowers. Playing tennis. Sure.

The ball whizzed back and forth until, eventually, it slammed into the net. The taller sunflower raised both leaves to its face in dismay, while the other punched the air in triumph.

The tennis ball rolled to Iris's feet. When she reached

down to throw it back, it just bounced and dribbled along the ground. The sunflowers now stood motionless and blank-faced and their leaves hung by their sides. The landscape was even parts of green lawn and blue sky, almost as if it had been designed that way.

Iris blinked.

She looked down at the feet-boots. They didn't feel warm anymore.

She moved towards the gate and the boots didn't stop her.

At first Iris only dared to walk. But the feet-boots let her go, so she broke into a run, away from the forest's edge. Only the grass minded, catching on her ankles as she raced past.

5

Iris slept on the unfamiliar bed, buried under the heavy quilt. She woke in the late afternoon, when the light slanting through the lace curtains had begun to pale.

The remains of a dream flickered at the edges of her mind. Something about being late for a test, and everyone in her class laughing at her because her head had inflated to the size of a large beach ball.

Iris lay still. Memories of the flight and her arrival and the ants returned. When she recalled the feet-boots, she leant out of bed to check if they were on the floor where she'd left them.

Nothing.

Iris didn't take much comfort from their absence. Deep down she knew that the boots and the man-sized sunflowers were only the start of it— *Bosque de Nubes* was hiding more surprises. She just didn't know what they were.

Before she straightened, Iris spied three letters gouged into the wooden bed leg. *J—E—N*. Her mum had used a sharp tool—a compass point or a Stanley knife—to scrape the beginning of her name, Jennifer. *It was a good thing Mum kept her maiden name*, thought Iris, *because otherwise she would have become 'Jen Chen'*.

The more she looked at the etching, the more Iris filled with irritation. Her parents hadn't prepared her for this trip at all. They'd given her confusing and conflicting instructions and, most importantly, they had not prepared her for what could *really* happen at *Bosque de Nubes*.

She found her phone in her backpack and waited for her messages to ping through, but there was nothing. Nothing from her parents, and nothing from Violet. *That's funny*, she thought, and then realised she had no reception.

Iris was pretty sure she'd seen an old-fashioned phone in the corridor, just outside her door.

'Hello, Mum,' she said as she walked there, in a far more sarcastic tone than she would dare to use in real life. 'I wonder if you forgot to tell me that the normal laws of nature don't apply at Aunt Ursula's house?'

The phone sat on a small table with a sunken seat, and instead of buttons it had a wheel. Iris lifted the receiver to her ear but the line was silent—no dial tone at all. A closer examination revealed that the phone wasn't plugged into the wall; its cord had been chewed, ending in a frayed, wiry mess.

Iris sat on the sunken seat and felt her irritation melt away. What was the point? They were too far away to help her, anyway.

To her left was the roped-off corridor, still pitch dark. It was newly sinister after the kidnapping-by-shoes.

Maybe it leads to a black hole, thought Iris. *A black hole where all the children who wandered off into the mists live.*

It was obvious that her mum had been deliberately keeping secrets from her about *Bosque de Nubes*, perhaps guessing correctly she would have been too chicken to come here if she'd known more beforehand.

Returning to her guestroom, Iris noticed a trail of paper arrows arranged on the carpet. After five arrows was a notice written in Aunt Ursula's elegant hand: *All Your Costume Supplies This Way.*

The arrows continued around the next corner to a small, disorderly space full of clothes. Pants hung next to skirts crammed next to dresses stuffed next to scarves. There were men's clothes and women's clothes, and a seething pile of shoes. In dim corners were shoeboxes, handbags, fairy lights and several broken tennis racquets.

Iris looked at the mess, already feeling tired. *What was the theme again?* Aunt Ursula wanted her to make a costume out of this stuff? She'd rather go back to bed.

A gong sounded in the distance downstairs. It struck again and again.

Iris left the wardrobe and went to the landing. Señor Garcia stood below in the lobby, dinner gong in hand. He was still wearing his navy uniform.

Aunt Ursula posed halfway up the stairs, her hand on her hip like a fashion model. Her long black dress trailed over the red carpet.

'Iris, are you ready?' she called out. 'Our guests will be here soon.'

Iris fell away before she could be spotted. It hadn't occurred to her there would be other guests coming to the party.

'I know you're there, dear! Iris?'

Reluctantly, Iris crept up again and looked through the balcony bars. When Aunt Ursula saw her she threw her arms up dramatically. The chandelier cast fragments of light upon her stricken face. *What was that under her nose?*

'Oh, Iris!' she cried, and sank into her pooling black dress. 'I'm melting, I'm melting!'

Iris couldn't see Aunt Ursula's legs. *It's a trick*, she told herself. *Don't fall for it.*

'Help me, oh, ohhh…'

Aunt Ursula tilted sideways and collapsed into a puddle of silk, her arms still held high. Her expression settled into a look of peace, eyes shut.

Iris stood up, mildly concerned.

Aunt Ursula opened one eye, then the other. She leapt to her very solid, unmelted feet, and squinted up at the balcony.

'Are you not dressed for dinner yet? Whatever is taking you so long?'

The ground-floor dining room was huge, not that Iris could see much of it with her head encased in an orb of white tissue paper. After drawing two eyes and a grinning mouth on the Chinese lantern, she'd poked some eyeholes as well, but they weren't much use once her head was inside. A pair of plain leggings and a striped poncho completed her outfit.

From the little Iris could see, she made out at least ten people seated at the long dining table.

'You are all a great disappointment to me, I must say. Except for young Iris, of course.'

Aunt Ursula's voice cut through the terrible music that was playing. It was worse than the jazz-rock fusion Iris's dad liked, which was saying something.

If you were only listening to Aunt Ursula talk, Iris thought distractedly, *you could imagine you were talking to a much younger woman.*

'When I was living in Paris,' continued Aunt Ursula, 'we used to have surreal dinner parties all the time, and the costumes were of a *verrryy* high standard. Iris will now give a speech about her artistic statement.'

'What?'

Iris was fast becoming claustrophobic inside the lantern.

Someone that sounded suspiciously like Jordi snorted from the end of the table.

'Stand up straight, dear, we can't hear you. Project your voice!'

'I don't have a speech prepared, and I don't even know what sorr...surry...whatever means,' Iris said. If she tried to stand again in this stupid lantern, she would surely fall over. 'I HAD A DREAM ABOUT HAVING A DISGUSTING GIANT HEAD. THAT'S ALL.'

'And that is an important lesson for everyone present, wouldn't you say?' pronounced Aunt Ursula. 'Disgust is my favourite emotion. I will explain what *surreal* means later, but dinner is now served. Iris, you may want to remove your head.'

The living guests were only seven in number, and the remaining 'guests' turned out to be mannequins. There were mannequins between Jordi and Marcel, and next to Señor Garcia. Aunt Ursula had glued a moustache on her lip. The room had been lit by dozens of lamps dotted here and there. There was a starched napkin folded into a swan shape and three plates in front of Iris, and more pieces of silver cutlery than seemed necessary.

Jordi waved discreetly from the far end of the table. His hair had been neatly parted and combed.

Iris waved back, relieved that he was there.

Her attention was then drawn towards the man and

woman flanking Aunt Ursula.

'You look amazing, sweetie. Just a treat,' the woman said in a nasal American accent. She was cheerful and plump and middle-aged, with waves of unmoving shiny red hair. Her costume was a homemade placard around her neck that read *Nightmare*. 'Puts us to shame, that's for sure.'

Iris flushed.

'I'm Shirley Dangercroft.' The red-haired woman extended her hand until Iris shook it, then pointed to her right. 'My husband, Zeke. We're the neighbours. A mile west. Hard to believe that qualifies us as neighbours.'

She turned to Aunt Ursula.

'And I believe I know what surreal means, *Mizz Freer*. It means "painting with a real sense of imagination", like your brother did. And it means "unexpected things", like your moustache.'

Aunt Ursula snorted and looked unimpressed.

Shirley's husband (grey suit, pink tie, no discernible costume at all) ripped apart a bread roll. He had a shiny face and head.

'I got no imagination at all, young lady, I'll admit that,' he said. 'Zero creativity too. Numbers, that's more my thing. Do you like maths?'

Iris shook her head. Charcoal paper streamers flew up as Elna stomped into the room, carrying a silver serving tray and wearing a pair of pantaloons made from brown feathers. A necklet of similar feathers, a hessian tunic and an owl mask pushed above her forehead completed her look. As if on cue, the cats-playing-violins music transformed into a series of cymbal clashes.

'Your help is as pretty as a painting!' exclaimed Shirley Dangercroft.

Elna scowled, but Shirley was not cowed in the slightest.

'I swear she belongs in one of your brother's paintings! I always wanted to own a real James Freer painting. Did I ever tell you that, *Mizz* Freer? It's been a dream of mine for a real long time.'

Aunt Ursula narrowed her eyes. She'd added a bowler hat to her formal black gown, and even with her fake moustache she was dignified.

'Dreams are not wants, Mrs Dangercroft,' she said. 'They are not objects or comforts. Dreams are the sneaky messengers of your mind. Dreams are the squirming pit of worms you refuse to look at when you're awake. Dreams show you everything you're hiding from.'

Zeke Dangercroft nearly choked on a piece of bread. 'Hiding? What would we be hiding from? Ha ha!' He poured himself more wine.

If it wasn't already obvious, it soon become *very* apparent from the sloppy way Elna delivered their soup bowls that she was in a filthy mood.

'*Gracias*,' Iris said when she received hers, copying Jordi. Elna glared at Iris as if she were to blame for the feathered pants.

The soup was lumpy and radioactive blue. Steam rose from the bowl.

Ursula took a mouthful. 'Dreams do not behave, my friends. And sometimes reality does not behave, either.'

Shirley Dangercroft forgot her shock and applauded.

'You're all so artistic, I swear. I feel so boring. There's so much—colour at *Biscuit Der News*.'

Shirley was right. The dining room walls and most of the furniture had also been draped in swathes of the charcoal-coloured paper. A random collection of objects hung from the roof, strung up with wool: silk roses, a wooden skittle, a toy dinosaur, a fish skeleton, a magnifying glass.

Marcel ate his soup and talked rapidly in Spanish to Señor Garcia, who was as silent as ever. Iris still felt wary around Marcel. He seemed as nice as Jordi, really—he also smiled a lot and used his hands when he talked—but she still remembered how furious he'd been on the phone.

Who, or what, could have made him so angry?

Iris could not convince herself to taste the blue soup, but Shirley Dangercroft had no such qualms.

'It tastes normal,' she babbled. 'Or I'm *almost* sure it tastes normal. But my eyes are telling me that it doesn't.'

Iris leant towards Aunt Ursula and spoke in a low voice.

'Aunt Ursula, is there a phone I can call my parents on? I was supposed to call them as soon as I arrived.'

In the back of Iris's mind was the idea that she could ask her parents to change her flight home to much earlier, if only she could describe to them exactly how freaked out she was by *Bosque de Nubes*.

'There is no phone.' Aunt Ursula didn't look at her.

It was hard for Iris not to sound annoyed. 'I found one upstairs.'

'Then use that one.'

'It's broken. There are blue and red wires coming out of the cord.'

'Ahh!' Aunt Ursula threw down her napkin in disgust. 'Reynaldo, darling, find the trap and go upstairs. That damn thing has been chewing on cords again. It favours the dark, so check the east wing first. You'll need a torch.'

'Is that the corridor near my room?' asked Iris. 'Why is it blocked off?'

'The floorboards are rotten almost all the way through. You mustn't go in there. Reynaldo is light on his feet and he knows where to step.'

Iris nodded. Señor Garcia bowed to the dinner party and left. Aunt Ursula slid back her chair and tapped her spoon against a glass.

'I wish to tell you of a vision I had last night.' Aunt Ursula had her honeyed stage voice on again. The lamplight erased her wrinkles. Zeke Dangercroft forgot his soup in an instant.

'I dreamt that I was flying above *Bosque de Nubes*,' Aunt Ursula said. 'Down the driveway towards the house. The garden was overgrown, weeds and vines everywhere, as if the forest were trying to take over the estate. When I got closer to the house I could see it was in ruins. The roof had fallen in, no glass left in the windows. I flew through the front door and there were trees growing inside, wallpaper ripped, vases smashed, paintings ruined. Leaves and dust everywhere.'

'It sounds awful.' Shirley Dangercroft dabbed her mouth with her napkin, looking upset. 'You have an outstanding property here. Outstanding. Full of history. If you're ever thinking of selling—'

'I couldn't decide if the sight of my ruined home was terrible or beautiful,' Aunt Ursula interrupted, and Iris made a mental note of Nightmare Shirley's comment. 'The dream may have been about hundreds of years from now… perhaps it was showing me the end of human civilisation? It's only right, of course, that nature will take over the planet again.'

Zeke Dangercroft snapped to attention. 'We got a letter this week, *Mizz* Freer, and Shirley and I have been wondering if you got one too. Perhaps that's what your dream is about?'

Aunt Ursula sat down again. 'I have no idea what you're talking about. I've received no letter.'

'It was those dratted property developers again, saying they could come and inspect our land, put a value on the place. It's only a matter of time before they start throwing pots of cash at people.'

Zeke Dangercroft was red in the face. He gulped more wine.

'We planned our European retirement for a very long time. I got no intention of moving on. No intention! If I wanted to be near a fancy country club, I wouldn't have moved here.'

Aunt Ursula peered at him. 'What is your opinion of golf, Mr Dangercroft?'

Zeke didn't have a chance to answer. Shirley Dangercroft had recovered from her sadness.

'One person sells to them and the rest fall like dominoes,' she said. 'You know how it goes, *Mizz* Freer. People forgetting what's important. Preserving the region. Preserving the *rustic atmosphere*. Aren't I right?'

Iris sat very still and tried to look as if she wasn't listening, when she was really filing all of this away to write in her notebook later.

This is exactly what my parents need to know, she thought, and then remembered that she was still supposed to be annoyed with them.

'I don't bother reading my mail.' Aunt Ursula sat very straight and her voice was stern. 'But if anyone thinks they are going to sweep in and take *Bosque de Nubes* from me, I have this to say to them. *Over my dead body*. Over my rotting, lifeless corpse!'

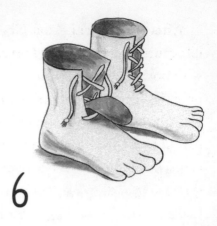

6

The second course was hamburgers, served on painter's palettes. They looked like normal burgers but were actually made from sponge cake, chocolate mousse and jam.

Everyone was too engrossed in their meals to notice the extra flick of Elna's wrist as she walked behind Iris. A small square of paper landed in Iris's lap.

Using the tablecloth for cover, Iris unfolded the paper. It was a photocopy of a painting, with the title written across the top: IRIS AND THE TIGER. This must be the other, more famous painting Elna had mentioned: a woman standing at a window, trees surrounding her.

Iris caught Aunt Ursula looking at her, and tucked the paper into her sock for safekeeping.

After the burgers, Aunt Ursula announced the 'invisible course'—a fur-covered tea set and a cake stand loaded with nothing but plastic dolls' heads. Iris had formed the impression by now that *surreal* meant super-weird.

Marcel, Shirley and Aunt Ursula kept up the farce of drinking air from furry teacups, but Zeke Dangercroft could not cope. The more wine he drank, the further he slumped over the table. Señor Garcia had still not returned to the party.

Finally, Jordi received permission from Marcel to slip up to Iris's end of the table.

'I can't hear anything over there.' Jordi frowned. 'It's boring.'

'I've been wanting to speak to you,' whispered Iris. 'You remember you offered to show me around? What kind of things did you have in mind?'

Jordi perked up. 'You are asking because you see something? Yes, you do! Tell me.'

Iris remained reluctant, until Jordi whispered, 'Something magics?' and raised his eyebrows meaningfully.

'There were these sunflowers,' Iris admitted, 'out in the forest, playing tennis. Have you seen them?'

She'd decided to keep things simple and leave out the kidnapping-by-boots.

'The big flowers on the tennis court? I know them!'

Jordi looked around. Aunt Ursula had coaxed Shirley out of her seat, and the two women were dancing to what

Aunt Ursula called 'free music'. Shirley was having trouble loosening up. At the far end of the table, Marcel was asleep with his chin on his chest.

Satisfied that no one was listening to their conversation, Jordi continued: 'I find them last summer! There are many magics, Iris. Maybe twenty or more. Really, you have no idea…'

Iris let out her breath. Her hunch had been a good one: ants and flowers and boots were just the beginning. She'd decided during the invisible course that she had to be brave and give *Bosque de Nubes* at least another day or two.

'Will you show me some other magical things? Could we go exploring tomorrow?' She hoped Jordi didn't have much to do on his weekend.

It was clear from the radiant look on Jordi's face that it wasn't only Iris who was relieved to have someone her own age to hang out with.

'You must come to our cottage, this is a definite plan. You will find it, the brick house. Ten o'clock?'

'Ten o'clock sharp,' replied Iris. Jordi looked confused. 'It means, yes. Ten o'clock and I'm really excited about it.'

'Me too. Sharp!' Jordi glanced at his snoozing father. 'I should get that old man home.'

Iris grabbed Jordi's arm before he could slide from his chair. 'You need to tell me: is it dangerous out there?'

'Where dangerous?'

'Well…' Iris bit her tongue again about the boots. Then

she remembered what Aunt Ursula had said earlier. 'Can you tell me, have there ever been any kids lost in the forest, when the mists come?'

'Oh, this.' Jordi patted her arm. 'You already hear about the famous mist? You don't worry. I tell you everything tomorrow.'

The house was cold and the giant chandelier dull as Iris made her way up the grand staircase.

Aunt Ursula had not let her stack any dirty dishes to take to the kitchen. Instead, they were going to close up the dining room and 'let the dishes fend for themselves'. Elna had rolled her eyes and rushed off to change out of her owl costume.

Iris would have gone straight to her guestroom if not for the light trickling from under the double doors at the top of the stairs. When she pushed a door open, it was as if something gently escaped—a puff of air, or perfume, perhaps.

The long narrow room was cloaked in dust and shadows. Opposite were floor-to-ceiling windows offering moonlight and stars. The walls were papered in apricot stripes; the floor gleamed.

It has to be a ballroom, Iris decided. Aunt Ursula had a maid and multiple chandeliers, so there was no reason why she wouldn't have a ballroom as well. Even though it was empty, it was easy to imagine the room full of people dressed in their finest clothes, dancing.

Iris had already slipped inside before she realised that the room wasn't empty at all.

At the far end was Señor Garcia, still in his suit, dancing. His arms were held shoulder-high to enclose his partner. His feet skimmed smoothly across the floor. He dipped his partner low to the ground, then spun.

Iris melted into the shadows near the wall to watch. When Señor Garcia turned again, Iris saw that he was dancing with a lamp, a tall standing lamp with a pink, fringed lampshade.

As he glided and dipped, Iris saw how Señor Garcia had left his shyness behind. She caught a quick impression of his face before he whipped his head around. His eyes were large and round.

Iris reversed towards the door—she was trespassing on a private moment. But as she did, her shoulder collided with a Roman figurine and set it rocking noisily.

Iris reached out and caught it by the neck, while Señor Garcia continued to dance. Iris glanced up. Paintings hung in neat rows on the wall. One painting in particular caught her eye.

Finally, Señor Garcia returned the lamp to a spot next to the fireplace, and his movements were once more deliberate and stilted. Eventually he disappeared through a darkened doorway at the far end of the ballroom.

Iris waited another minute before breaking her position. There may have been dozens of paintings on the wall, but the one she was interested in was easily the largest; it showed green grass, yellow petals and blue sky.

The tennis court was much better tended in the painting. The net hung tautly; the umpire's chair was a bright slatted white.

Uncle James had painted a large sunflower growing at either end of the court and their golden petals stuck up like crowns against the bright blue sky. The title, *Courtly*, had been etched along the bottom edge, and next to it a scribbly signature: James Freer.

Apart from their size, the sunflowers were ordinary. Even so, there was something slightly *off* about them.

Or do I only think that because I know they're not ordinary? Iris wondered. *People thought Uncle James painted from his imagination, but there was more to it than that.*

Iris checked the main door, and then the other doorway that Señor Garcia had taken. It led to a small area used to store wineglasses and serving trays. There was a bench, a shelf and a dumbwaiter's hatch—and no way out, only an open sash window. The drop to the ground was at least five metres.

Iris was torn between looking at Uncle James's paintings for longer, and figuring out where Señor Garcia had gone. In the end she returned to the ballroom. But it was too dark to see Uncle James's paintings properly.

As soon as that thought crossed Iris's mind, a row of lights sprang into life along the wall. The shades were upturned hands holding glass orbs—and so realistic it was as if someone had dipped human hands in gold.

The paintings were an extraordinary blur of landscapes, an old-fashioned car, a man with two faces, a monstrous plant chasing a maid through the hallway. There were three formal portraits of an insect, who posed in human clothes and had googly eyes, long antennae, and six spindly legs. Uncle James had signed these with just his initials: *J.F.*

A painting hanging nearby flickered. It showed an underwater scene, a rush of water, bubbles and waving water plants. There were two pink legs in the lower right corner. The legs kicked—once, twice, three times—before swimming out of view, beyond the edges of the painting. One second they were there, the next they were gone.

Iris's first day in Spain had already been so long and strange that she barely flinched. Still, she had trouble believing that any of these other paintings could be real.

The next painting along showed a grand piano, twisted like a black stallion rearing in alarm. Mutant ants crawled across the keys and onto cream sheets of music. The sheet music fell in an arc to the floor and ants were everywhere.

For a moment her head swam. Iris felt crawling up her spine, as if the ants had migrated there. She had not entirely believed Jordi when he'd said there was nothing dangerous out there.

There was no way she could ignore it now.

'There you go,' she said out loud, with just a hint of

hysteria, 'the paintings are real, the paintings are real, the paintings…'

Because no one was there to comment, her chant turned into a song, and she marched around in circles while she sang. It had been a long day, and now her ankle was itching.

I better not have been allergic to those boots, Iris worried.

But when she scratched her ankle, she found a folded-up piece of paper in her sock. It was the photocopy of *Iris and the Tiger* that Elna had smuggled to her during dinner.

Iris examined the copy with interest. Her namesake, Iris Freer, was older in this painting, and wore her hair differently in two big bunches on top of her head. She stood at a wall with a circular window, her hand on the sill, her face turned slightly towards the front. All around the wall was a dark forest; through the window was a choppy sea. There were no tigers anywhere.

Uncle James must have called it *Iris and the Tiger* for a reason. The more Iris absorbed the painting, the more she felt that there were clues in it: messages meant especially for her.

If only I could see the real painting, she mused.

An idea flashed in her mind. The underwater painting now showed only a rush of brown water and weeds. The legs were completely gone.

What if there had once been a tiger in the painting, but it had already wandered off?

She pictured a golden head with golden eyes and pricked

ears, somewhere in the house. A striped body prowling down the curling staircase, out the front door and into the forest. Tail flicking as it moved beyond the edges of the painting and out into the real world. The tiger, doing exactly as it pleased, not caring in the slightest about the rules that should have kept it on the canvas. A tiger that was somehow linked, not to Iris Freer but to *her*, Iris Chen-Taylor. Somehow it was *her* painting and her tiger.

Iris didn't move for minutes, for fear of disturbing her new idea. Ever since she'd started high school, it had been plainly obvious to her how very ordinary she was. This was a sign, though, that things didn't have to be that way.

She was going to find the tiger.

Iris didn't sleep in the following morning. A cock crowed as she lay in bed, her head full of colours and shapes from the previous day—and her dreams overnight, which were made up of a dozen whirling paintings with tigers at the centre.

Be honest, she lectured herself. *Is it crazy to think there's a tiger at* Bosque de Nubes?

Back at home, in her regular life, it would be clear that her imagination had spun out of control. But here, in the land where paintings became real, it wasn't the worst idea she'd ever had.

She couldn't decide if she should be thrilled or scared. Tigers were not to be trifled with. They were beautiful and dangerous and unpredictable. Iris hoped she was brave enough to solve the mystery.

When Iris emerged from her room, she was met by a knee-high statue with a basket on its head: a squat stone man with an enormous belly, big ears and poking-out tongue. The basket held breakfast—a pile of long Spanish doughnuts dusted in icing sugar called *churros*.

An envelope had been tucked under the basket.

It was another message from Aunt Ursula, who seemed unable to deliver any messages in person.

Enjoy your churros, delivered by the god of rain and lightning, it read. Then underneath, *A Game of Art, to be played in twos.*

Iris chewed on a doughnut. Her mum would have a fit if she saw how much cake she'd eaten in the last twenty-four hours.

The back of the envelope had been sealed with a blob of red wax. There her great-aunt had scribbled another message:

P.S. Your parents called while you were asleep and insisted on talking to you. I informed them that you were far too busy to bother with idle chatter.

P.P.S. I've gone on a few errands. Please help yourself to anything in the kitchen. Or anything in the house.

Iris allowed herself a small smile. Aunt Ursula wasn't all bad.

It would be best not to speak to her parents straight away. They'd never believe the magic stuff, so she would have to leave all that out. And then what would be left? Rumours about developers? Nosy neighbours?

Iris tucked the envelope into her jeans, along with the photocopy of her painting. It felt good to have her own reason for being in Spain. She would have to work on the tiger mystery and her original mission at the same time. She wouldn't be able to avoid her parents' phone calls forever.

Spaced around the balcony were eight doors, plus the one to the guestroom. Iris knew what lay behind a few of them—the ballroom, the lounge room, the walk-in wardrobe. That was just the start, though. *Four* corridors led from the balcony, including the forbidden east wing with rotten floorboards. It was impossible to estimate how many rooms there might be in the mansion.

Iris finished the doughnut. If the *Iris and the Tiger* painting was in one of those rooms, she wanted to find it. But the size of the house wasn't even the biggest problem. She knew nothing about art. If she were going to find the tiger she would have to understand the painting.

Iris tried one of the unknown doors.

It opened onto a library with walls lined with bookshelves, leather armchairs and several lamps. At the far end of the room were wooden cubbies full of masks and musical instruments, paper skeletons and other knick-knacks.

Iris ran her finger across some book spines. They were

dusty, but the library looked used. There was a round indent in the armchair as if someone had sat in it recently, and a stack of magazines piled haphazardly next to it.

The magazines were old. Iris flicked through one called *Harper's Bazaar*, from 1956. There weren't any photos of celebrities without makeup, or actresses falling out of limos and flashing their undies.

Instead there were articles about lipstick and setting hair (whatever that meant), and a story about a famous Hollywood actress who married a European prince. At the end of the magazine there were 'Society' pages that showed people at fancy parties.

A photo caught Iris's eye. Two women stood close together, laughing. The caption read: *Women in Art Lunch. Iris and Ursula Freer delight in the elegant surrounds of the Hotel Pierre ballroom.*

Iris Freer was tanned and outdoorsy and easily recognisable from the greyhound and the tiger paintings. The young Aunt Ursula had familiar pale skin and dark hair.

There were all sorts of other books on the shelves: astrology, gardening, romance novels, woodworking manuals. A shelf of art books contained a slim catalogue with Uncle James's name on it. The words were in Spanish, but the paintings were full-colour.

Iris gasped when she found *Iris and the Tiger*. It looked so different in colour. Iris Freer's curly hair glowed yellow. The trees were a hundred different shades of blue and purple. In this version, Iris could see that the sea contained shadowy shapes, and one of the trees had an eyeball planted in its trunk.

Iris squinted. *How strange.* The green eye bulged out of the tree. It even had eyelashes.

She examined the painting avidly. There was *still* no tiger visible. It seemed like a bigger riddle than ever.

So this photo was taken after the tiger already disappeared from the painting…and the same with the copy Elna gave me. Iris rubbed her temples. Her brain hurt from thinking it through. *Could there be a copy somewhere with the tiger in it? And could the tiger come and go from the painting?*

When Iris left the library, the god of rain and lightning statue lay tipped over on the balcony, the frayed end of the telephone cord nearby.

'Are you the Thing that eats the telephone cord?' asked Iris, but received no answer, of course. The doughnut basket had rolled into a corner.

All the lights were on, but the house was deserted.

Iris was most of the way down the stairs when she felt the prickle of someone, or some*thing*, near her. There was nothing behind her on the staircase. Iris kept walking, aware of a gentle clacking near her on the lobby tiles.

She passed through the kitchen to the back door. The air stirred around her ankles. Iris stilled her breath, daring to hope that the tiger had come to her already. The thought made her feel faint. But all she saw on the patio was a wan shadow of a dog.

The greyhound-shaped shadow wagged its tail, and then ran on five legs down the patio stairs—fast!—and across the dusty yard, all the way to an overgrown corner of the building that appeared older than the rest.

Iris followed, excited to encounter the dog from the painting, and willing to forgive it for not being her tiger.

A glass greenhouse clung to the main house, seemingly held together by only moss and ivy. The greyhound shadow slid around on the greenhouse door.

Iris put her face to the glass, but it was so grimy she couldn't see inside. She tried the handle, but the door was locked. The dog shadow wagged its tail.

'I can't, dog, it's locked,' said Iris. She started to walk off, but the shadow wouldn't follow.

'Come on, let's go meet Jordi. You can tell me which is his home.'

The shadowhound wouldn't budge. Iris wished she knew its name. She soon gave up on him and crossed the yard.

Jordi and Marcel's cottage was in a secluded corner of the garden, a red brick building with white shutters and a miniature picket fence.

Jordi opened the door only seconds after her knock.

'*Hola*,' said Iris, as she'd practised.

The cottage was simple inside, with wooden floors and

white walls. The lounge room contained a couch and a TV and a dining table and not much else. The walls and mantel and floor were bare, except for a wooden cross above the TV. Iris wasn't sure where to stand.

Marcel poked his head out of the kitchen and waved an oven mitt. The doorways were too low for him.

'There's been a change of plans,' Iris said in a low voice, once Marcel had gone. 'I've realised something. Something *big*. I found out something new about the magic.'

She held out the catalogue that she'd taken from the library.

'You probably know some of these paintings.'

'Actually,' Jordi said, 'I have never really look at Señor Freer's paintings. I don't know anything about art.'

'It doesn't matter,' Iris said. 'I don't know anything either, but last night I figured it out, after the party. I found some paintings in the ballroom—do you know there's a ballroom upstairs?—and found out that all of Uncle James's paintings are real. Like, he's famous for painting things that aren't meant to be real, but the thing is, *they're all real*. There's a painting of the tennis court flowers in the ballroom, and there's others as well. A piano, and...'

Jordi's forehead was scrunched. 'Everything in this book is out there? So, it's like a map for the magics?'

Marcel came into the room, put two mugs down on the table, then left.

'Sort of. I don't know. It doesn't tell us *where* all these things are, but it does tell us what *might* be out there. What do you think?'

Jordi showed her a page of the catalogue. To her surprise Iris saw that he'd picked out the underwater painting with the tiny disappearing legs.

'I know where this is. It's easy, I take you there now.'

Marcel returned with a plate of small round rolls. He looked with interest at the catalogue. Iris hadn't decided if she was still scared of him.

Marcel put his finger down on a page and said something in Spanish.

'What did he say?'

'He know this one.'

It was a painting of an old-fashioned car that had four furry, clawed feet instead of wheels.

Marcel said something urgent.

'We must not find this car,' translated Jordi. 'He is being...' Jordi flapped his hand, which Iris had noticed was what he did when the right English word wouldn't come to him. 'When people have some rule that is stupid, like do not put your umbrella open inside?'

'Superstitious.'

It made no sense to Iris that people in Spain were superstitious about cars with animal feet. Marcel sat on the couch to lace his boots.

'Actually, I am interested to find this car,' said Jordi. 'It is very cool.'

Marcel obviously understood the tone of his voice, because he let go a stream of sharp-sounding words.

Jordi held up his hands. 'Okay, Papa, okay. I won't do it.'

Feeling awkward, Iris picked up a mug and drank. She'd thought it was tea, but it turned out to be coffee. She let her mouthful dribble back into the mug, and no one saw her. She bit into a roll.

'Delicious,' she said loudly.

Marcel said something else and Jordi replied.

'He says you look as if you can have Spanish blood,' Jordi explained to Iris. Iris shrugged. She couldn't be bothered going into the usual boring family explanation (father from Hong Kong, mother from Australia, blah blah), but it was a nice mistake. It hadn't occurred to her that her dark hair and eyes might allow her to pass for Spanish.

Marcel left the cottage with his cap in his hand. Jordi turned to Iris.

'You are not liking coffee!' he laughed. 'So now we go match painting with place, *si*?'

Iris nodded. It was on the edge of her lips to tell Jordi about the tiger, but something, she wasn't sure what, held her lips closed.

Jordi flicked through the catalogue again—pausing at the car page.

'We bring this book with us. I think this could be a very dangerous mission.'

He looked extremely happy as he said it.

8

Iris and Jordi walked down the driveway. After the roundabout and the roses and the straggly hedges came the forest. It didn't look as threatening in the sunlight.

'The magic, that's just at *Bosque de Nubes*, right? Not everywhere in Spain?' Iris asked breathlessly. She had to work to keep up with Jordi.

'I know only magics in here.' Jordi indicated the boundaries of the estate. 'Road over there, big road there, golf course, fence. There is old stories about the magics in this place. My *abuela*, my grandmother, she knowed them. This way.'

Iris followed Jordi down a furrowed track. There was a high brick wall beside them. The trees were thin here.

'I can't figure out why Aunt Ursula wouldn't warn me.'

'Papa says never discuss the magics with Señorita Freer. When he come first to *Bosque de Nubes*, she tell him: *No talking*. In front of others pretend you do not see. I think she would tell you the same.'

Iris shook her head. 'Do you have any idea where the magic comes from?'

Jordi raised his eyebrows, shrugged, waved his hands.

'I don't know. Some talk of a…sorry, I can't think of English word.'

He paused.

'I remember now—witch! There are some old stories about the magic and the mists and a witch. It's make-believe, though, you know, stories for babies.'

Iris remembered her first glimpse of the woods. They'd looked exactly like the kind of place you'd find a witch's house. *But maybe that's an immature thing to think.* Iris pushed the idea away.

'How long have you lived here?' she asked. If Jordi could live around the magic every day, then it mustn't be so bad.

'I was born here. Papa and Mama moved here when they got married.'

It was the first time Jordi had mentioned his mother. He read Iris's face instantly.

'My mother does not enjoy being a mother. So she go to the city, where there are no horses and not so many trees.'

'Oh,' said Iris. She hadn't been fishing for extra information.

'Now I only get a card on my birthday and a few times a year Papa likes to yell at her over the telephone.'

'I see,' said Iris. She remembered Marcel's angry voice and red face from the tomato patch. 'My mum must have visited before your parents moved here—did you know my mum came here when she was a girl? Uncle James was still alive then. Did you ever meet him?'

'He died before I was born. I think my father, he know him a little.'

Jordi unlatched a gate in the wall. The paint on the gate was so dry and crackly it powdered Iris's fingers white.

'Now you have come to my house, we are friends,' he said in a matter-of-fact way.

'Oh. Okay.'

Iris was taken aback, but pleased. That was quick. She couldn't help thinking of Violet—when was the last time she'd been to *her* place? It had been Easter holidays, and only for one day.

On the other side of the wall was a pond circled by a path. Insects buzzed around lavender bushes. A weeping willow leant towards the water.

They sat down on a pair of rocks and regarded the pond.

'What do we do now?' Iris whispered.

'We wait.'

The pond was murky with weeds. Iris flicked a bee away from her head. The water didn't look very deep. She wasn't sure what she was supposed to be looking at.

After a while, Jordi stood and threw bits of gravel into the pond. 'Sometimes this can work.'

'Hey, Jordi, are there any wild animals in these parts?' Iris tried to sound casual. 'Deer and goats and other things?'

Jordi held up a finger, suddenly alert. *'Espera.'*

A ripple disturbed the centre of the pond. Small circles moved outwards into bigger circles. Something leapt from the water into the air. Iris blinked at the wrong moment and missed it. Whatever it was, it had been small.

The something flung itself into the air again. It had the silver scaled head and body of a fish and a pair of pink naked human legs. It was *tiny*.

Iris grabbed Jordi's arm. 'Is that what I think it is?'

Another fish-with-legs leapt gracefully from the water and splashed down again. Then another, and another.

'Mermaids!' Iris finally got the word out. Jordi laughed.

Three, maybe four, mermaids flashed across the pond's surface. Iris tried to get a proper look at them, particularly the bit where their fish body merged into human legs, but it was impossible. Iris found herself laughing too. It was all so strange: paintings that came to life.

She wanted to do a happy dance. *Fish with legs! This is evidence that my theory about the tiger isn't completely loopy.*

After a few minutes the water grew still again. The sky's reflection settled on the surface.

'That's it?'

'They don't play for long.' Jordi sounded pleased, even though he'd probably seen the mermaids plenty of times.

'They were the opposite of what they should be.' Iris was reluctant to look away from the pond. 'Usually when people have imagined mermaids, they make it the other way. Human body, then a fish's tail.'

'I know.' Jordi brushed his hands and took a serious tone. 'It was…how is it…disappointment? It was disappointment when I first saw this, not to see the chest of a woman.'

'If you want to see *that*, there's a billion naked statues in the house. I can show you.'

Jordi snorted so hard he started coughing.

Iris was pleased with her comeback. That had literally never happened before. She'd known Jordi for a little over a day, they were officially friends and she already felt more comfortable with him than with people she'd been at school with all year.

Jordi and Iris walked back up the dirt road, followed by a faint rustle. Iris turned her head. The five-legged shadowhound rippled on the brick wall, trailing them at a safe distance.

When they reached the front gates, Jordi slapped them and made a low metallic clang. Up close Iris noticed the words *Bosque de Nubes* twisted into the iron among a cloud pattern. A colony of nearby birds tweeted furiously. The tree cover was still thick, all the way up to the gates and perimeter fence.

'Iris, you know this painting is called after you?'

Jordi held the catalogue open at *Iris and the Tiger*, trying to match it up with the landscape in front of him. Iris had told him she wanted to find the eyeball tree, but still hadn't mentioned the tiger.

'It's named after Uncle James's wife, actually. She was also called Iris.'

'This is not near here. We go further, into the trees, far from the road.'

Iris sighed. 'You know your way around, right?'

'I go all the time. Mostly on horse. You want to go on horse?'

'Umm, let's sit a while and then we can decide.'

Iris slipped off her backpack and lay down in a grassy dip. The grass was cool and slightly damp. Her jeans crinkled.

She pulled out the envelope from Aunt Ursula and broke the seal. Jordi sat next to her.

'*Instructions For Exquisite Corpse, A Most Famous Game*,' Iris read out loud. 'You want to play this? It's a game from Aunt Ursula.' She read further. 'Her artists buddies used to play it in the olden days. Before TV and computers.'

A car zoomed along the highway outside.

'Corpse means dead person, *si*?' Jordi was certainly

interested. 'It is a murder-mystery game?

'I don't think so.' Iris scanned the instructions. 'It's more of a drawing game. I don't have a pen, though.'

Jordi pulled a texta out of his hoodie pocket. 'I like to write my name on fences,' he explained.

'That's called "tagging" back home.'

Iris took the texta. She was terrible at drawing, and Art was her worst subject, by far. There was an extra bit of paper in the envelope that had been folded into four lengthways.

'Right—I draw a head on this top part of the paper, without letting you see what I'm doing. Then I'll fold the paper over to hide it, but make sure I leave a tiny bit of the neck showing. Then you'll draw the arms and body, and fold the paper again. Then I draw the legs, same way, then you draw the feet.'

Iris referred to the instructions again.

'Aunt Ursula says that the most important thing is that we draw without thinking about it. She calls it Automatic Drawing. Got it?'

'Let me go first. I want to draw the head.'

Jordi used the catalogue to lean on and Iris rested. After a while she became aware of the sound of the texta scraping against the paper, and the wind rustling through the treetops. She wondered if the shadowhound was still near.

'I am wondering two things.'

It was strange hearing Jordi's voice without seeing him wave his hands about.

'One—why does Señorita Freer bring you here? And two—why does your parents not worry when you are far away? That is not usual.'

'*Un*usual. That is unusual,' Iris corrected him. 'Well, maybe Aunt Ursula is lonely, and that's why she wants me to visit.'

'But your parents? Why do they remove you?'

Iris was tempted for a moment to tell Jordi the truth.

'Maybe they're worried about Aunt Ursula too,' she said eventually. 'Anyway, I was glad to get away.'

'*Por qué?*'

'I don't know.' Iris heard the paper crinkle. 'School's not much fun at the moment, I guess.'

'It is your turn.'

Iris opened her eyes. The top quarter of the paper had been folded over, leaving two short lines.

Jordi turned away and Iris pressed the texta to the paper. She left it in place so long an inky blotch formed. She started with a circle, and no plan for what she would draw.

'It's really hard to turn off my brain,' she said.

It was true she had come to Spain to please her parents, and to try out being a spy, but it was equally true that she needed to escape school for a few weeks.

'I don't have this problem,' said Jordi. 'For me it is hard to turn my brains *on*. I do not look forward to high school.

I am not good student, but I do not have to be there forever. After three years I move to Costa del Sol and I become a jockey. I must be fifteen years old for this.'

Iris drew a set of eight skinny arms, waving about like a Hindu god. She filled the body in with meaningless squiggles.

'You've already figured out what you want to do for a job?'

'Of course.'

Iris tapped Jordi on the shoulder.

'Anyways, I do not know how you can be sad when you ride the kangaroo to school every morning.'

'Oh. You realise that was a joke, right?'

'You no telling me the truth?' Jordi looked teary. His voice went high. 'There is no riding the kangaroo?'

Iris felt awful, until Jordi could no longer hold a straight face. Iris punched him in the arm.

Jordi drew the legs fast, without talking. When it came to her turn, Iris drew the feet as quickly as she could, not sure if what she was doing could really be called automatic. Wasn't there always thinking? Even thinking about *not-thinking* was thinking.

'I'm done,' she said.

Jordi unfolded the drawing and laid it flat.

Their Exquisite Corpse had the head of a bear, the body of a spider and two scaly legs that ended in a pair of sneakers. Jordi's legs almost looked like they belonged to a

Chinese New Year dragon, and Iris wished she'd known so she could have given their creature kung fu slippers rather than running shoes.

'You can draw,' she accused Jordi. 'Your bits are much better than mine.'

Jordi had given the bear's head shaggy tufts of fur. Its eyes glistened. When Iris looked at it, she was almost convinced that such a crazy mixed-up creature could exist.

'Why did your mama not warn you about the magics before you come to here? You say she come here?'

'I'm not sure that she knows about it,' Iris said, folding their drawing. She'd thought about it a lot. Could her mum have been that blind to the magic? Or was she just a really, really good liar?

9

Once they'd left the driveway, Jordi's behaviour changed. No longer relaxed, he scanned the trees as if there were snipers in them. Then he took off sideways through the light scrub. Through the leaves Iris saw him drop into a commando roll.

Iris had agreed to venture into the forest, but as a safeguard insisted that they keep the outer fence within sight. *What if the mists come, and we have to spend the night in the forest?* Iris had learnt some bush survival techniques at school camp, but she wasn't sure they would be much use in Spanish woods.

'You're going to tire yourself out!' she called. She didn't want to imagine how much Jordi would carry on if he knew she was searching for a tiger. He was already convinced they were in an action movie.

'We travel for days into the heart of the jungle.' Jordi flicked his hair out of his face. 'Maybe there are landmines. Probably we are going to explode.'

Iris tried not to sigh. Jordi pulled out his texta and scribbled his name on the next fence post.

This part of the forest had already been touched by autumn—there was orange and yellow on the trees, and crunchy dead leaves underfoot.

'Jordi, have you ever seen the mists?'

A car revved on the nearby highway. Spanish people drove fast and had nice new cars.

Jordi answered by dropping to the ground. He grabbed Iris's ankles, tripping her up so that she sank.

Her knees slammed into the dirt.

'Ow! What did you—'

Jordi shushed her. He crawled on hands and knees towards the fence, beckoning frantically for Iris to follow him. They peered through the rusted iron bars.

A red car was parked on the other side of the highway. A man and a woman unpacked equipment: an instrument on top of a yellow tripod and a heavy-looking suitcase.

'They are here before,' Jordi whispered.

He made Iris crawl further along the fence.

'I see them here, at the home of Dangercroft, and near the school. When Papa see them he use bad words. Words he usually keep for my mother.'

The duo seemed to be debating where to set up their equipment. The woman held a tablet and scrutinised the screen. They were young and dressed like they were about to play golf. In all the excitement about the tiger, Iris had forgotten that she was also supposed to be looking out for these sorts of things.

'What do you think they doing?' Jordi asked.

'They're surveyors. I'm pretty sure. They measure and map the land.'

Iris had seen surveyors before, in the city. Her dad worked with them sometimes, when people wanted to build the buildings he'd designed.

'But in Australia they would wear fluorescent vests and work boots and drive a van,' she explained. 'Maybe these ones are hiding what they are doing.'

'Why are they here?'

'I've heard there are people that want to buy all the land around here. Property developers, I think. The Danger-crofts were talking about it last night. They think someone wants to build a big resort or country club.'

Damp seeped through Iris's jumper. The ground smelt musty and rotten.

'No wonder Papa doesn't like it.' Jordi looked worried. 'He works for the Freer family for over twenty years. He has done a lot for Señorita Freer. I think he hope to grow old at *Bosque de Nubes*, to keep the cottage and die there. This is the land of his childhood.'

'We should tell Aunt Ursula that people are measuring her land.' But what Iris really meant was that she needed to get a message to her parents.

'Papa really won't like this.'

'I don't think you need to worry. Aunt Ursula will never let anyone get their hands on *Bosque de Nubes*. She said so last night—and I could tell she meant it.'

But deep down Iris knew there was still a problem. Aunt Ursula wouldn't live forever, and then what would happen?

'My stomach is so empty. Empty and sad.'

Not only did Jordi not cope well with being hungry, he was also anxious to speak to his dad.

From the driveway's edge, Iris could see black trunks staggered far into the distance. The sunshine made dappled patterns of light and shade, so it was easy to see things that weren't there. Or not see things that *were* there.

'Will you remember which parts of the estate we've searched?' Iris asked.

Jordi didn't answer. He stood at the edge of the drive-way, looking into the forest.

'What is it?'

'Do you see it?' Jordi took a step forward.

'See what?' Iris's insides flip-flopped. The birds stopped twittering.

'I see something.'

'You're imagining things.'

'I see it *there*. Something running.'

Iris saw a fallen tree covered in moss, rocks, a carpet of ferns. Jordi reminded her of a cat stalking a bird.

'We should look.'

Jordi jumped into the ditch that ran alongside the driveway. Iris had no choice but to follow. For a shortie, Jordi sure could move.

'Slow down!'

Jordi had already made it over the fallen tree and was heading up a hill almost fifty metres ahead.

A splinter pierced her palm when Iris belly-flopped across the tree, but there was no time to stop. Jordi crouched on the steep slope ahead, holding on to a trunk for balance. He gave Iris a hand up.

A battered old black car was parked in a clearing at the top, partially covered in fallen branches and leaves.

'Didn't your dad tell us not to go near a car?'

Iris was out of breath, but Jordi had already run ahead and was trying to force the driver's door open. Iris glanced up and felt swoony. The towering trees were swaying like the masts of ships. The sky was still light.

Jordi had his face pressed to the car window. The car was wedged so tightly between the trees that Iris couldn't imagine how its driver had parked it there. It was broken down, not dangerous.

'It's even older than the one Señor Garcia drives,' Iris said.

She tried to remember what had been unusual about the

car painting, but Uncle James's paintings were all starting to blur together.

'We can go for joyriding.' Jordi walked to the rear of the car.

Iris doubted if the car still worked. It was huge and rusty.

She pulled at the weeds growing over the bonnet. They came away easily, exposing two round headlights, both cracked. The bonnet was torn across the front, leaving jagged bits of metal sticking into the air.

'I think this car was in an accident.'

The old-fashioned silver grille on the front of the car had prongs that attached at the top and bottom, all different shapes and sizes. They looked like—

Iris stumbled backwards.

Like teeth!

The grille was a grinning mouth. The headlights were two blinded eyes.

'Iris! Iris!'

Iris dragged herself from the scarred face.

Jordi crouched next to the car, inspecting the passenger door. There was a deep dent in it, but that wasn't what had his attention.

Instead the wheel was a large foot, as big as an elephant's and covered with matted brown fur. Claws dug into the dirt. Iris glanced down where she stood—and realised the claw was now moving towards her.

'*Dios mio!*'

Jordi leant on the car to stand up, and gasped.

'It's warm,' he said. 'Like alive.'

Jordi's and Iris's eyes locked. They turned and ran—and didn't look back.

10

After Jordi had left, Iris parked herself in the climb-ing tree again, hugging a branch sloth-style. Her brain would surely explode while she was in Spain. Every time she remembered the feral car, a cold liquid shiver ran through her.

In a way, its discovery was good. It was more likely than ever that a single tiger could be hiding on the estate. A tiger was much smaller than a car, and stealthier too.

The back door clanged. Iris didn't even lift her head.

The tiger could be out there, she thought, *but could it be found?*

Perhaps she was going about it back-to-front. The answer might lie with the subject of the portrait: Iris Freer.

There was a crash and a high-pitched cry of distress.

Iris leant out of the tree.

Señor Garcia had dropped a large cardboard box on the patio. He crouched to recover the spilled contents. Iris spied several wigs and piles of red, silky fabric.

Señor Garcia shuffled to the greenhouse. He set the box down and retrieved a small object from the windowsill. A key. Señor Garcia unlocked the door and took the box inside.

Iris waited.

After a moment or two, Señor Garcia emerged from the greenhouse again, this time carrying a flat rectangle wrapped in a white sheet. He staggered up the stone path, stopping halfway to rest. Iris felt sorry for him. His arms were little more than twigs.

The sheet fell aside at the corner, revealing a picture frame, a floral pattern, and a dark patch of paint, perhaps the top of someone's head. Iris slid down the trunk. He would be in big trouble if he had dropped a painting.

But before she could reach him the back door opened. Aunt Ursula rushed out, wiping her hands on an apron. She said something to Señor Garcia and he began shaking as if he was laughing. Aunt Ursula patted his shoulder. Together they took the rectangle up the stairs and through the back door.

Iris watched them, pressed against the tree trunk. She felt a little uncomfortable spying.

Señor Garcia returned to lock the greenhouse door

and put the key on the windowsill. Aunt Ursula came out again with a plate of biscuits. She put the plate down on the outdoor table. Then she drew her arm back like a baseball pitcher and threw an imaginary ball across the yard. The shadowhound raced across the dirt, skidding about in a cloud of dust.

Elna had taken the night off. And because Aunt Ursula could not be bothered to set the table, dinner was served in the kitchen. It was the first time that Iris had been properly alone with her great-aunt for more than a few minutes.

The kitchen at *Bosque de Nubes* was even more old-fashioned than the rest of the house, with worn benches and a chequerboard floor. The only stove available was the pot-bellied sort that you had to feed with wood. A kettle sat permanently on top.

'Did you get a chance to play the Exquisite Corpse game?'

Aunt Ursula poured herself a sherry and Iris a fizzy tangerine drink. They sat on stools at the bench. The over-head light wasn't bright enough to banish all the shadows.

Iris pulled out their drawing and smoothed it flat. She pushed aside a tray of biscuits to make space. The biscuits had an odd appearance—each had a leaf pressed into the dough, and some also had pieces of bark. Iris hoped she wouldn't be offered one. She couldn't help but think of all the fairytales where children were fattened up with delicious cake. Perhaps it was Jordi and his talk of witches that had brought it to mind.

Aunt Ursula put on her reading glasses and examined their bear-spider-serpent creature. She'd changed into silky pants with a long Chinese-looking embroidered jacket over the top.

'All the good bits belong to Jordi,' Iris said. 'I can't draw, and I don't understand art.'

'You don't need to. Children understand art. It's grown-ups who know nothing about it.'

'But I was wondering, Aunt Ursula, why do artists like this game so much?'

'You've played it. What do you think?'

Aunt Ursula went to the old green refrigerator, her silk jacket dragging on the floor.

'Well, adults don't usually play games. The worst thing about high school is that no one plays games anymore. There isn't even any play equipment.'

Iris's brain was urging her to ask about the magic, or to tell Ursula about the surveyors, but her mouth had other ideas.

'The boys still play football and basketball at lunchtime,' she went on, 'but the girls sit on the steps and talk. And all they talk about is clothes and TV and boys. It's boring.'

Aunt Ursula dished up two wedges of frittata onto their dinner plates.

'In my experience, girls often pretend to be older than

they really are,' she remarked.

That's school exactly, Iris thought. *Everyone pretending constantly, even Violet.*

'Did you ever do that, Aunt Ursula?'

For some reason this made Aunt Ursula chuckle.

'I'm terribly sorry, Iris, I'm not laughing at you.' She spooned out the salad. 'Actually, I did pretend this, once upon a time. When I first visited my brother in Paris at nineteen, I hid how little I knew of the world. I was constantly worried that someone was going to discover how green I really was. It became a game in itself: wearing the right clothes, going to the right parties, having the right opinions. It was very tiring.'

Aunt Ursula handed a knife and fork to Iris.

'What were you and Uncle James doing in Paris?'

'James was supposed to be studying at the big-deal art academy, but he'd dropped out. Everyone predicted he'd come home with his tail between his legs, but instead he started selling lots of paintings. I was sent there to talk him into returning to Australia. War was brewing in Europe and my parents were desperate for him to return.'

Ursula leant in. Her skin was paler than usual. Iris could trace the faint outlines of veins across her forehead, and there was a smudge of yellow and pink along her hairline.

'No one suspected I had a secret plan. I knew from his letters that James had befriended some famous artists. I thought it was all absolutely marvellous and I was determined to join the gang. I had no intention of talking James into returning home!'

Iris could hardly imagine how Ursula had dared to be so brazen. She could never lie about something so big.

'You asked why the painters played the Exquisite Corpse game?' Ursula continued. 'This gang had a lot of games, just as children do. But the games had a serious purpose. It was a way for them to get in touch with a different part of their minds, a trick to make buried ideas and thoughts bubble up to the surface.'

Iris felt more confused than ever.

'Aunt Ursula? I have a question about Uncle James. Or it's about one of his paintings, *Iris and the Tiger*?'

'Ah, yes, of course.'

'What I want to know is: which room is it kept in? I found a picture of it in a book, but I'd love to see the real thing.'

'Oh, the painting is in Barcelona. It's worth too much to have here. The art gallery there keeps it safe. *Bosque de Nubes* is very...demanding. It's so difficult to maintain things as they were.'

Iris's face grew stiff with disappointment. Uncle James had pictures in galleries all over the world; it had been stupid to think his best one would be hidden in the countryside.

'Of course. That makes sense.'

Her eyes started to sting, as if she were going to cry,

just like a baby would. *Why is it so important to me? It's just a painting.*

'I suppose we could go to Barcelona and visit it,' Aunt Ursula said. 'It's not so far to drive. It would take careful planning, of course.'

'Only if you want to.' Iris cut up the frittata into a dozen small pieces instead of crying.

Aunt Ursula sported a familiar faraway look. 'I yearn to see some of the other paintings again, naturally,' she said, 'but we could run into some problems. It sounds as if she's genuinely interested...what would it be like to spend a whole day with a little girl...?'

Iris stopped cutting. 'I am still here, you know.'

It wasn't like Iris to snoop, but she was literally led to it. All she'd wanted was to watch the sunset from the patio.

The shadowhound had other ideas.

It ran in front of her, rushing at her legs and then retreating. When it galloped right through her Iris felt a cool breeze.

'I've got too much on my mind. Go away. I don't want to play.'

The dog wouldn't give up. Somehow it made itself darker and clearer than usual against the marble paving. Iris remembered that the hound had belonged to Iris Freer, when it was alive and more than a shadow.

'What are you trying to tell me, dog?'

Iris followed the shadow to the greenhouse. She stood on tiptoes and felt for the key on the sill.

Above the greenhouse roof was a row of windows belonging to the main building. The windows were curtained, but as Iris watched, the curtains twitched.

Her fingers grasped the key finally. It was an old key, with a clover-shaped head. The curtains had grown still.

'Will you come with me?' asked Iris, but the shadow-hound flickered away.

The door opened smoothly. Iris had expected to walk into a messy storage shed but instead found herself in a painting studio. There were easels in a dozen shapes and sizes, canvases leaning against walls, and jam jars stuffed with paintbrushes.

She locked the door from the inside, in case anyone should come by and try the doorhandle. The box that Señor Garcia had carried in was next to the door, spilling dark red satin and fake hair. One of the wigs was long and black and curly.

Perhaps he puts them on his favourite lamp. Iris smiled.

A few strands of ivy had burrowed through the windowpanes. Other than that, time had stopped in the studio. The easel at the centre held an unfinished painting. A cup and saucer sat next to Uncle James's palette. It was freaky to imagine that one day Uncle James had walked away from his easel and never returned.

There was a trestle table against the wall, bookshelves,

a rocking chair, and a huge mirror at the end of the room.

Iris flicked through a sketchbook on the trestle—no tigers. Further along there was a stack of loose papers.

The first sketch was upside down, and showed a girl's face in profile. Even though it was just a few lines, the drawing captured perfectly the way the girl bit her lip. She looked nervous. She looked familiar.

Iris turned the sketch the right way up. Her own face gazed back at her.

A sudden gust of air snatched the paper out of her fingers and the entire stack tumbled to the floor. Cold fear gripped Iris's throat, as if the ghost of Uncle James were in the room. A paintbrush rolled off a table and hit the floor.

Iris ran for the door. When she got there, though, red liquid had started to pour through the doorframe. The red thickened and dripped; within seconds the trickle had turned into a flow. A curtain of blood-red paint poured over the door and nearby walls. The doorhandle was slippery and still locked.

Iris spun.

Colour gushed down the other three walls of the studio: blue, white, yellow. Paint spatters hit the floor and formed pools. A wave of primary colours covered the scattered paper on the floor. The room had grown dark.

Iris started for the far end of the room and slipped over. Fumes filled the air. When she tried to stand, she fell again.

The Spanish police would mail her body to her parents,

and when they opened up the box they'd find paint in her throat and ears and mouth, and then they'd be really sorry.

When Iris felt a hand on her shoulder, it wasn't a ghost but Aunt Ursula, her face a blurry pink blob.

She let Aunt Ursula pull her to her feet. The tide of paint had receded, leaving no trace behind. Iris looked down at her sneakers and jeans, and the only marks were grass and mud from the forest floor.

11

The morning was bright and finally Iris's head felt clear again. From the guestroom window she viewed the veggie patch and the orange grove and the stables and the rolling hills. It would have been prettier than a picture, except for the two brown and pink feet-boots lined up beneath her window.

Iris shuddered and clambered from the windowsill. There was not a chance she would put those shoes on again.

Her notebook lay open on her bed, covered with frantic scribbled notes from last night. Iris read over her account of what had happened in the studio and began to suspect that she had overreacted. It seemed unlikely now that she'd seen a sketch of her own face, and there was no way she could have drowned in paint.

Aunt Ursula had been extremely kind afterwards, tucking Iris into bed with a cup of chamomile tea. She had even lent Iris her own childhood teddy bear, a tattered, faded thing with no ears. Iris didn't tell her that she was too old for soft toys, and Aunt Ursula hadn't asked why Iris had been in the greenhouse studio in the first place.

The locked studio, Iris realised. *I tried to escape through the door and couldn't. Yet moments later Aunt Ursula appeared in the room.*

Iris pushed the thought aside. It had been a confusing incident, and she felt terrible about snooping. Not telling Jordi or Aunt Ursula the full truth was taking its toll.

She lay on the bed and punched out a text message to her parents:

> *Many rivals but house not so great.*
> *Y do U even want it?*

She hit send, but the screen froze and she couldn't tell if anything had happened.

Señor Garcia dropped Iris in front of the Sant Joan public library so that she could continue her research into James and Iris Freer and the paintings.

On the way to town, they'd passed Jordi and Marcel riding the horses. Jordi had been wearing a shirt and tie, which had looked all kinds of strange.

Where are they going?

Soon after, Iris's phone had got reception and started pinging with text messages from her parents. She looked at the first few, and then couldn't bear looking at the rest. She could already tell that her mum's messages were getting more and more frantic.

Iris hurried through the library doors, tugging at the silk scarf she'd tied around her neck in an attempt to look more European.

There was a payphone in the foyer. Iris felt in her pocket for the phone card Aunt Ursula had given her.

Somehow she remembered the international dialling codes and the line began to ring. There was a click and a crackly pause. Iris's throat tightened.

'*Hellooooo?*'

Iris's mum had a completely different voice she used to answer the telephone.

'Mum, it's me.'

'Iris! We've been trying to call the landline, and I can't figure out what's wrong with the lines in Spain, but we've only got through once and then Ursula was in one of her "challenging" moods and refused to put you on—'

'I was asleep, Mum. The jet lag was bad...'

'You were supposed to message us when you arrived, and we waited—no message! We only just got one now. Your father is beside himself, you know how he gets.'

'Sorry, Mum, it's been kind of...busy here...and weird.

You didn't tell me Aunt Ursula would be so—'

'I never pretended that your great-aunt was anything other than completely off the planet. It's how these creative types behave.'

Iris took a deep breath.

'Mum, say our family, I mean, say *I* inherit *Bosque de Nubes*...' By now Iris could say the Spanish words smoothly. 'And say there are people already living here, people other than Aunt Ursula. It would be pretty unfair, wouldn't it, if we made those people move? Don't you think?'

Iris heard her voice get echoey and knew that she'd been put on speakerphone.

'What other people?' boomed her dad. 'Hello Iris. You mentioned rivals in your message—what did you mean by that? And the problems with the house? Are there cracks? Water damage?'

'Iris, what is the state of Aunt Ursula's health?' interrupted her mum. 'She must have a nurse at her age, surely? Is she in a wheelchair, or does she have a walking stick?'

Iris already regretted making the call. *'Hi, Iris,'* she said under her breath. *'How are you going over there? Are people being nice to you?'*

'We can't hear you, darling,' said her mum. 'Stop mumbling and speak clearly.'

Iris smushed her scarf against the mouthpiece. She was beginning to fill with panic over her parents' questions. If she kept talking they might sense that she'd been distracted from her main mission. 'Oh, oh, you're breaking up, I can't hear you!' She held the phone away from her mouth. 'I can hardly hear anything. *Schhhhchhhkkk.*'

And then she hung up.

The library was small but modern. It had a central courtyard, and a corner for chess. Even though she was pretty sure it was the same as the libraries in Australia, which anyone could use, Iris hurried into the privacy of the book stacks.

Beyond the shelves were old people reading newspapers and kids in beanbags reading comics or playing computer games. Along the back wall was a row of computers.

Two days ago Iris had been desperate to check her emails, but now it didn't matter much. She was sure Violet hadn't bothered to email her, as she hadn't even texted.

She approached the front desk. The librarian wore a sparkly fox brooch and looked friendly.

Iris handed over the scrap of paper that Marcel had helped her prepare. He had written in Spanish at the top: *I need to find some information about—Spanish animals* and underneath Iris had added 'James Freer' and 'Iris Freer'.

The librarian set Iris up on a table across from an old man doing crosswords. She gave Iris a folder full of newspaper clippings and some books.

Iris spread everything in front of her. She wasn't sure what she was looking for.

The books were all in Spanish. She flipped through a book about local animals. The pictures were mostly of mice and squirrels and rabbits, but there were a handful of interesting cat-like creatures.

The largest was an Iberian lynx. It had satellite dish ears and spotted fur. *EXTINTO* leapt out from the text. One photo showed the lynx ripping apart a bird with its sharp teeth. Iris flinched.

The old man, who wore a full three-piece suit and had no teeth, set aside his crossword and began rifling through Iris's folder. She watched from the corner of her eye as he found an article that excited him greatly. He held the paper out to her and chattered in Spanish.

Iris shrugged apologetically, trying to convey with gestures that she couldn't understand. She slid her chair closer and picked through the clippings.

There were old photos of the Freer mansion and an obituary for Iris Freer. The picture must have been taken during the war: she wore army-type clothes, and carried a medical kit.

The old man's voice grew louder. He seemed more excited, and also sad. Iris could tell from the tone of his voice that he was saying something like: *Oh, terrible, terrible*. He flapped the paper again, so Iris took it off him.

It was a front-page news article, yellowed with age. A

smudgy photo showed a car accident: a familiar black car wrapped around a tree. The attached report was unintelligible, but the headline contained the name 'Iris Freer' in block letters, and the word *muerta* too.

Iris looked closely at the photo. It was easy to imagine teeth on the mangled car, clawed feet too. She felt sick.

When she left the library, Iris still had almost an hour before Señor Garcia was due to pick her up. She followed the road until she came to the town square. Whenever she passed a villager she imagined that they, like Marcel, thought she was Spanish.

Iris sat on a bench and watched a group of old men play a game similar to bowls. The photocopied news article was stored in her backpack. Jordi would never want to go near that horrible car again once he'd seen it.

Who knew that history could feel so heavy? she thought.

Iris took in the whitewashed buildings lining the square and the olive trees along the road and the sun overhead. There was a red car with dust on the windows parked nearby and, behind it, tables and chairs and umbrellas belonging to a café. It looked very similar to the car she and Jordi had seen yesterday.

Four people left the street-side café and gathered behind the red car. The stoutest wore a shiny grey suit that matched his shiny face and head.

Zeke Dangercroft.

Two others were the surveyors, still dressed as if they

were playing golf, and the final member of the group was an older man with silver hair.

Mr Dangercroft shook their hands in turn, grinning widely. Then the two surveyors crammed into the hatchback; the older man beeped his sports car across the way. When they'd gone, Zeke Dangercroft turned to cross the square and his grin slid off his face.

Iris jumped to her feet, a bunch of pigeons jumping with her. Mr Dangercroft flinched, but quickly gathered his wits.

'It's my new Australian friend! *G'day*, Iris!'

Iris was not fooled by his forced cheer. She could not be bothered with small talk.

'Who were you having lunch with?'

Zeke Dangercroft wiped his forehead. 'You Aussies don't mess around, my word.'

'No, we don't. Those people have something to do with those letters everyone's been sent.'

Iris could barely believe how bold she was being. She was getting better at faking being braver than she really was. After all, she had survived the boots and the tennis flowers and the mermaids without having a heart attack.

'Well, young lady, you'd be correct about that, yes.' Mr Dangercroft lowered his voice. 'I went fishing for information and I did not like what I found.'

Iris watched Mr Dangercroft very carefully. 'And what was that?'

'Oh, complicated business matters,' he said, waving his hand. 'Those men are not very high up. They're salespeople, if you will.'

He mopped his forehead again. Iris had once read that sweating was a classic sign of lying, but it *was* a warm day.

'I understand,' Iris said. 'You mean that they've been hired by someone with more money and more power, who is making all the decisions. But what is *that* person trying to do?'

'A theme park,' Mr Dangercroft admitted. 'A kind of "arty" one, with rides and buildings based on famous paintings, including your great-uncle's. That was as much as I could find out. It means major construction, though. Clearing the forest. Land for car parks, new roads, hotels, a man-made lake.'

'A theme park? But wouldn't that cost millions of dollars?'

'Oh, they've got millions of dollars. Or Euros. It's an international group of companies, some Spanish, some Chinese, other countries as well.' Zeke Dangercroft was totally out of puff. 'But it makes no difference to me and you should tell your aunt that, please. I said we wouldn't sell, no matter what we're offered. Shirley wants that to be clear. She wants *Mizz* Freer to know we can be trusted.'

He pulled an envelope from a pocket inside his jacket.

'Actually, it's lucky I ran into you, Iris. Your aunt has agreed to sell Shirley one of her brother's paintings. This is a cheque for the deposit. If you could pass this safely into *Mizz* Freer's hands, I would be most obliged.'

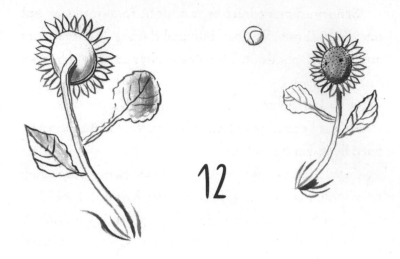

12

Back at *Bosque de Nubes*, Iris helped Señor Garcia carry the shopping into the house. The driver still hadn't spoken to her, not that it mattered. Iris had realised that all of Señor Garcia's nods were the same yet each said a different thing.

They met Elna, who was dragging a full garbage bag across the lobby with many complaints.

'She's waiting for you,' she said to Señor Garcia. He hurried towards the kitchen, almost skating on the polished floors.

Iris laid down the shopping to help Elna. Even between two of them, the garbage bag was heavy. It was full of knobbly objects that pressed uncomfortably into Iris's palms.

'Señorita Freer forget he cannot be in two places and one time,' Elna said. They bumped the bag over the stairs and to the front door. The plastic slipped through Iris's fingers.

'What's in here?'

Elna did not seem to hear Iris's question. 'They are best friends, if you can believe.'

Today Elna had her hair French braided and was wearing gold hoop earrings so big they brushed her shoulders.

'Okay, little Australian, I take it from here. *Gracias.*'

Iris let the bag go. It was torn along the side. Squished silver ends and grubby plastic screw tops bulged out— hundreds of paint tubes threatened to spill everywhere.

Iris remembered Zeke Dangercroft's cheque in her pocket.

'Where's Aunt Ursula? I need to give her something.'

'Señor Garcia knows where her little hidey-hole is, but I do not. I stop asking questions because I never get any answer.' Elna gestured. 'Give to me.'

Iris hesitated. Elna raised her plucked eyebrow until Iris handed the cheque over. Elna blew her a kiss before pulling the torn plastic together and hoisting the rubbish over the threshold.

A new picture hung next to the front door. Someone had rescued the Exquisite Corpse drawing from her bed and smoothed it out. Their bear-spider-serpent-jogger creature was transformed into real art now that it was in a frame.

Aunt Ursula had typed a small cardboard sign. *Drawing by Furious Yellow*, it said. Iris was filled with an unfamiliar glow.

Below the picture a half-moon hall table was littered with mail: junk flyers, a postcard signed 'Sophie Adria (Ernesto and Carmen's daughter) xx', a number of bills, and other letters in both English and Spanish. There was nothing from anyone about a theme park.

Iris sent her parents a text summary of everyone she'd met so far in Spain, including the Dangercrofts and the mysterious property developers. She stood in the one far corner of the patio where she could sometimes get reception. Afterwards, she lay on a banana lounge in the garden as the sun beat down.

Iris scrolled through the photos on her phone. There were lots of selfies of her and Violet that now seemed to be lies. Violet was so busy these days with netball practice and dance class and new friends that there wasn't any time left for Iris. Even when they *did* hang out together, it wasn't the same as it used to be. There was so much already that Iris had to tell Violet about Spain, but she suspected that she was going to go home and say nothing. They used to tell each other everything.

At what point did a person have to admit that their best friend was no longer their best friend? Did they have to make it official at a meeting?

Iris scanned the grounds for the shadowhound. She hadn't seen it at all that day. She stood up and headed towards the stretch of grass.

There was no one in the vegetable garden and there was no answer when Iris knocked on the door of Uncle James's studio, not that she would have dared go in. The kitchen and the dining room were deserted, and Elna's cleaning cart was nowhere to be seen.

She went to the living room to look at the old photos on the wall. They were of barbeques and dances and exotic locations. In one party pic, Aunt Ursula wore a pirate hat, and Uncle James had his face covered with a Zorro mask. James hadn't been bad-looking. Iris could imagine the girls at school squealing over him.

On a mantelpiece, Iris found a photo of her mum and Aunt Ursula. It had been taken on their trip to the beach, but in this photo Aunt Ursula had removed her hat and sunglasses. She wore a wide lipsticked smile and looked exactly the same, as if thirty years hadn't passed. She hadn't aged a bit.

Iris climbed onto the windowsill behind her bed and pressed her face to the glass. The gardens below were dark, the woods beyond even darker. The sun tickled the distant mountains before sliding out of sight.

Jordi and Marcel led Turrón and Miró across the backyard. Iris itched to run downstairs and make another time with Jordi to explore, but it was after 9pm—probably too late to visit.

The windows above the greenhouse studio glowed orange. As Iris watched, a shadow crossed one. More shadows appeared, thin lines that stretched and lengthened, as if there were a tree inside, trying to get out.

Iris's breath fogged the glass; she wiped it clear. The shadows were gone.

There was a knock at her door and Elna carried in a TV tray.

'Supper?'

Iris reversed from the window. 'Did you give the envelope to Aunt Ursula?'

'She is nowhere in sight, but I leave it on her bed.'

Elna arranged a bowl of tomato soup and a plate of toasted cheese sandwiches on the coffee table.

'What does Aunt Ursula do all day?' asked Iris.

'So tomorrow you go to Barcelona?'

'I guess so.' Iris picked up a sandwich. *Elna never answers my questions*, she realised. *No one here answers my questions!*

Elna didn't leave. She stood and twiddled the ends of her hair instead.

'What is it?' Iris spoke with her mouth full, but her mum wasn't exactly there to tell her off.

'Your fingernails are terrible.'

Elna prised Iris's hand off her sandwich. Elna's own

fingernails were pearly white with fluorescent orange tips.

'You cannot go to the city like this. I paint them for you.'

'Elna, how long have you worked for Aunt Ursula?'

'It has been five years. Sometime I think I will never escape this house of crazy people. What colour you want? I go get it.'

Aunt Ursula had said that Elna was new, Iris thought. *But five years is a long time. In five years I'll almost be finishing high school.*

'Purple?' she said eventually, trying to be polite. 'I like purple.'

13

The sky was lavender when they left *Bosque de Nubes* for Barcelona the following morning. It was cool outside, but Iris wound the car window all the way down anyway. The house looked stately as they pulled away.

The forest was all twisted shadows in the morning light. As they gathered speed around a corner, Iris glimpsed something moving in the shadows. Where the forest was darkest, there was a momentary glint, down low.

'Wait!' Iris jolted up in her seat.

'What is it?' asked Aunt Ursula. But they had already zoomed past.

Iris looked through the back window but there was nothing more to see. There *had* been a shape, though, she was sure of it. A dark object moving fast—really fast—through the trees. It had been close to where Jordi had said he'd seen something.

After they'd crossed the first lot of mountains, the rain started: first soft, then hard.

'It always rains in late October.'

Aunt Ursula pulled a book and her reading glasses from her bottomless handbag. Her cheeks were plush and rosy, as if she'd been using special face cream.

'Don't worry. I'd bet my little finger it will be sunny by the time we reach Barcelona.'

Craggy mountains rose beside them. Terracotta-roofed towns clung to the lower slopes; below were the neat lines of vineyards.

As Aunt Ursula had predicted, the rain soon stopped and the sun came out. Every now and then Señor Garcia would silently point out something of interest: a farm, a donkey, a bridge spanning a ravine.

Once they'd reached the outskirts of Barcelona, the houses and roads seemed to go on forever. The streets started big, then got narrower. Houses were replaced with apartment buildings. They drove down a wide, busy road, surrounded by scooters and delivery vans and taxis.

The car eventually stopped outside a gargantuan white building with walls that rippled like shaken bedsheets.

'Meet us outside *El Angel* at two o'clock,' Aunt Ursula said to Señor Garcia. Iris caught a glimpse of Señor Garcia's heavy eyebrows and straight nose in the rear-view mirror before she hopped out of the car.

'What will he do while we are in the gallery?' asked Iris.

'I suspect he'll head for the hills, though he won't tell me. That creature has as many secrets as I do.'

Aunt Ursula swept Iris across the plaza, through a door, and past the front desk of the contemporary art museum. The ticket clerk waved them through.

They walked up a ramp to the next level, then kept going. Aunt Ursula's rings struck the handrail musically and Iris glimpsed the plaza below. The people walking across it had already been reduced to specks.

Iris pointed them out. 'Ants.'

'Exactly,' Aunt Ursula agreed. Today she was wearing a multicoloured Mexican skirt and a flowing blue kimono. Depending on how she held her arms, she either resembled a moth, a witch or a kite.

Iris stared as they passed a group of students sketching a sculpture on the next landing. It was a large metal spider perched on long spindly legs, its tiny round body suspended above their heads.

The cool kids were easy to pick out, at the rear of the pack, looking bored, refusing to sketch. Maybe high school was the same all over the world.

Iris and Aunt Ursula walked the rest of the way in silence until they reached the exhibition on the third floor, with the title *Convulsive Beauty* printed across the entrance arch.

Sounds like the name of a heavy metal band.

'I have it on good authority that your painting is in here,' Aunt Ursula said.

Iris's nervousness peaked as they entered. There were paintings on the walls, sculptures hanging from the roof, glass displays of magazines and sketchbooks, and even a film projecting in a nook.

Iris kept close to Aunt Ursula as they paused at a colourful painting of a woman with monkeys sitting on her shoulders.

'I met her when I lived in Mexico,' said Aunt Ursula. 'A wonderful woman.'

'Aunt Ursula, is all this stuff surreal?' Iris still wasn't sure she understood what made Uncle James and these other people's art different from others.

'I suppose so. But that's just a label, Iris, I wouldn't trouble yourself about it. Think of this art as surprising and odd, as dreams can often be.'

Iris had never dreamt of monkeys, but she liked the painting a lot. She could have looked at it for quite some time and not get bored.

Aunt Ursula did not let them linger, though.

'It's not in here,' she said, ushering Iris along. 'Ah! Now we're cooking with gas!'

The next room was as big as the ballroom, and crowded. A tour group gathered around a guide with a flag. A whole corner had been devoted to Uncle James's work.

Iris tried to peer through the throng. She saw something familiar in the gaps between bodies.

'Oh, Aunt Ursula, look!'

The insect portrait was larger than any in the ballroom—and the funniest yet. The bug wore a judge's wig and a bored expression. He raised a wooden hammer, as if about to deliver a verdict.

Iris scanned the walls until she found *Iris and the Tiger*. It was surprisingly small, no bigger than a tea towel, and it was housed in the plainest of wooden frames. She felt a momentary flush of disappointment.

In the painting, the original Iris stood at the window. Her hair made a golden halo around her pensive face, and her stripy brown jumper looked fuzzy enough to touch. She was barefoot. The trees had thousands of individually painted leaves, and patterned trunks.

Iris was no longer disappointed. The painting was small but perfect. She imagined herself standing at the circular window and looking at the churning ocean.

Iris Freer looked calm, but the purple trees were threatening and the sea dangerous.

Maybe Uncle James painted this after a bad dream? Iris thought, remembering Aunt Ursula's words. Or perhaps it was an example of automatic art, like the Exquisite Corpse game—he had just painted whatever came into his head.

Aunt Ursula still stood near the entrance, talking to an old man in a beret and a younger woman. The woman was clasping Aunt Ursula's hand, almost kissing it.

Iris got to work quickly, with her notebook, a pencil and a magnifying glass. She started with a section of sea, holding the magnifying glass close. A stern gallery attendant came over to check she wasn't touching the canvas.

Iris checked every millimetre of sea until she was sure there wasn't a tiger hidden in its depths. After that she moved onto the forest, and then the very edges of the canvas. The eyeball tree appeared more intriguing than ever.

The tour group filed past.

'An exquisite work,' said a loud English voice behind Iris. 'The famous painter James Freer at the peak of his power. He was nobody until he came to Spain, but something here agreed with him.'

'Perhaps it was like that blues singer, Robert Johnson,' chimed a softer voice. 'Maybe Mr Freer sold his soul to the devil in return for talent.'

The louder woman was instantly dismissive. 'It had something to do with the climate. And *love*.' She said *love* as if she was talking about a hideous disease. 'That's his wife in the painting. He was very nearly disinherited because of her. She was a communist.'

'Those artists were all communists, weren't they? Ooh, I do adore these insects. Most comical.'

'There's quite a fascinating story about them. The insect portraits were only discovered after Freer's death. They'd been stored in a farmhouse attic somewhere. Absolutely dozens of them. No one had any idea he'd been so obsessed.'

'How fascinating.'

'They sold for a great deal of money at auction. Galleries and collectors all over the world scrambled to secure one.'

'Do you think there are more out there?' The second woman grew excited. 'Can you imagine if we found the genuine article in a dusty junk shop?'

The two women moved on, their heels sharp on the floor.

Iris packed her things into her backpack. Her suspicions—that the tiger had disappeared from the painting long ago—had been confirmed. But even though she'd *looked* as hard as she could at *Iris and the Tiger*, she had the sense that she still hadn't *seen* it clearly.

Aunt Ursula had ended her conversation by the door and was now contemplating another painting by the Mexican monkey woman. Her kimono wings were slack and she seemed a little sad.

Perhaps she misses all her old friends, Iris mused. *They were sure to be scattered around the world or dead.*

Iris wandered into the last room, which had a wall of touch screens. The school group from earlier were scrolling through digital versions of the artworks.

Iris sat down at a screen. She ran through the alphabet until she came to 'F'. To her surprise, there were two entries for Freer: *FREER, J* and *FREER, U*.

Iris clicked on *FREER, U* and a headline flashed before her:

Sister fools art world with bold prank

There was a photo of a young woman flanked by security guards. Iris tapped and zoomed in. It was Aunt Ursula, dressed in a men's dinner suit.

Iris scrolled down to the text.

In 1951, New Yorkers were the victims of an elaborate hoax at the opening night of James Freer's exhibition, *Self*. Attendees were engrossed by Mr Freer's speech on the meaning of many of his paintings, only to later discover that they had in fact been addressed by the artist's younger sister, Ursula.

Those present were bamboozled by Miss Freer's impersonation, with many reporting that they had no idea they'd been talking to a young woman. It later transpired that Miss Freer had hung several of her own amateur paintings among her brother's without detection. Many art collectors said they could no longer trust the gallery or the artist. Mr Freer did not make an appearance at the exhibition opening.

Iris leant back from the screen. After the melting-on-the-stairs incident, she probably shouldn't be surprised that Aunt Ursula had been pranking all her life. Young Ursula wore the most triumphant look on her face in the photo, as if she was pleased to have been caught.

The hoax was a funny story, but Iris felt more unsettled than ever.

Is there something else I should be paying attention to? she wondered. She slid off the stool to find her great-aunt.

14

Lunch happened underground, in a restaurant where the walls were cold bluestone and lanterns cast shards of light. It could have been any time of day at all, because there were no windows. Everyone else in the restaurant was an adult; Iris was careful to sit up straight and use her cutlery correctly.

Aunt Ursula looked pale and tired. She moved her food around her plate without eating.

'What did you think of your painting, young Iris?'

'It was beautiful. The colours were brighter in real life.'

Iris stabbed a croquette. She was incredibly hungry.

'But I think I'm missing something with it. Was it definitely painted at *Bosque de Nubes*? The trees look right, but not everything is there, so...'

'Aha, I get your point. You're wondering about the sea, aren't you?'

'Oh. Yeah, the sea.'

'The coast is hundreds of kilometres from *Bosque de Nubes*, so how could there be an ocean in the painting?'

Aunt Ursula fished in her tapestry handbag and drew out a flat case that held a cigar. She lit it and began puffing clouds of dirty smoke into the air.

Iris glanced around. No one else in the restaurant was smoking.

'As I said, everyone was very interested in dreams at the time. In dreams, water symbolises emotions. So I think that James was telling us how he felt about Iris. Then, of course, there's the tiger—'

Iris drew a sharp breath.

'I'm sure you've noticed there's no tiger in the painting. That's typical James…'

Iris waited, but that was the end of Aunt Ursula's sentence.

'Are there any tigers near *Bosque de Nubes*?' she asked, eventually.

'No. Mountain goats, maybe, and I'd say definitely some wild boar. I think the title was a practical joke. But tell me, Iris, in your opinion, is *Iris and the Tiger* really James's best painting? Or perhaps you find the insect portraits more interesting?'

Iris tried not to get annoyed about the change in topic.

'Hang on—do you mean there was *never* any tiger in the painting?'

'That's correct, yes.'

Iris slumped into her seat. She felt deflated.

Aunt Ursula has no idea how important the tiger is to me. I thought this was something I could solve on my own. She tried to rally her spirits. *I'm sure Uncle James wasn't playing a prank by calling it that. He had to have a reason.*

She remembered another practical joke.

'I found something else interesting at the gallery.'

Iris showed Aunt Ursula the photo she'd taken with her phone of the touchscreen.

The older woman's face brightened. 'Where was that?'

'It was on the computer.'

With her head bent down, Iris saw that Aunt Ursula needed to dye her hair again.

'Why did you do it, Aunt Ursula?'

'Oh, well, my brother considered it to be very funny. And I was…rather angry, actually.'

'What about?'

'It was like this: the male artists back then were a club, and women could be part of it, if they were someone's wife or girlfriend. Or you belonged if you were a muse—that is, if you were pretty enough to photograph or paint. I was none of those things.'

Aunt Ursula rearranged the folds of her kimono.

'I also wanted to make great art—I wanted it more than anyone. But people wouldn't take me seriously.'

'How did you do it?' Iris asked. 'You fooled everyone!'

Aunt Ursula puffed on her cigar.

'I'm a very good actress. I was always asked to perform in art films despite my plain looks. That silly Elna of ours, she wants to be on one of those terrible soap operas, but she appreciates nothing of the craft.'

Iris crossed her fork over her knife.

'Was Uncle James disinherited because of a communist?' she asked, carefully.

That made Aunt Ursula laugh.

'Oh my! All the skeletons in the closet are rattling!' She tapped the cigar against her teacup. 'That's only half true. My parents were displeased when James eloped with Iris, but it had nothing to do with communism. They didn't approve of her family background, that's all. James didn't lose his inheritance. Not like your father.'

'Oh, oh yeah. Exactly.' Iris did her best not to fidget.

'It was a terrible choice for your father to make. Please his family or marry the woman he loved. Quite noble, when you think about it. Giving up his share of the family fortune—a considerable fortune, if what I've heard is correct.'

Iris tried not to flinch at the idea of her parents and their noble love, but in the end she couldn't help it.

'Gross,' she said. Ursula did not disagree.

It had been so long since Iris had heard her phone ring that she almost didn't recognise the sound. She scrabbled through her backpack. The elevated terrace was crowded with tourists taking photos and admiring the view.

'Hello?'

'Oh. Iris. Well, this is a surprise.'

'Mum, you rang me—how can it be a surprise?'

'I've tried, of course, but it's never gone through before. This line is very clear.'

'Aunt Ursula and I are in Barcelona for the day. We're at Parc Güell.'

Iris sat down on the long mosaic bench that snaked across the terrace. She could see treetops and mottled roofs and the towers of the Sagrada Família, a famous cathedral. They were high above the city. Parc Güell was a cross between the Botanic Gardens and a carnival and a fairytale palace. Some of the buildings looked as if they had been made by elves.

Iris waited for her mum to speak.

'Now, we got your message, Iris. It's all very interesting, and your father and I want to thank you for the work you've done.'

Why is Mum being so weird? Iris wondered.

Aunt Ursula was in the distance, trying to coax a parrot to feed from her hand. She looked smaller, somehow, outside the confines of the estate. Even further away was Señor Garcia, awkwardly holding a parasol.

'We think the key lies inside Aunt Ursula's home, among the people closest to her.'

'Um, okay. Well…I mean what about the developers? They're more important than the housemaid, aren't they?'

Iris heard muttering and interference.

'I don't think you should bother yourself with those outside concerns,' said her mum. Again, there was muttering.

'Mum, if Dad has something to say, why don't you put him on?'

'Your father and I are in agreement that you should leave the developers alone and concentrate on what's happening inside the house.'

'Sure.'

Iris did not agree, but she knew not to mess with her mum when she used that tone. She felt like someone had poured quick-setting concrete over her.

'Okay, then, thanks for calling, Mum. Aunt Ursula needs me. I better go.'

Only after she hung up did Iris remember that she'd wanted to ask about the Chen family fortune.

Iris didn't try to stay awake on the drive home. The light ebbed out of the sky as they left Barcelona. Headlights swooped out of the darkness and away. Raindrops spattered the windows again.

'Somebody should have warned you about what you

would find at my home.'

Iris opened her eyes. Aunt Ursula was propped on the seat next to her. Her face was powdery-white, her hair jet-black; she looked straight out of a silent movie.

'It gave you a big shock, whatever happened in my brother's studio,' she said. 'And all your questions about the paintings—I know you know.'

Iris tried to reply, but she wasn't as awake as she thought she was. Aunt Ursula pushed herself upright.

'I was very nervous about having a child visit. Jordi is different, I've known him forever. But I had no idea how to entertain a young girl. I fear I got it very wrong, Iris.'

Iris recalled the over-the-top dinner party on the first night, and Aunt Ursula pretending to melt, and her ridiculous poem and all the cake. And those were just the non-magical things.

'I love your house,' she said eventually. 'I love Spain. This is the biggest adventure I've ever had. But how come my mother didn't tell me how unusual *Bosque de Nubes* is?'

Aunt Ursula half-opened her eyes. Streetlights lit up her face at intervals.

'Your mother couldn't see anything. There's no magic inside her. I know you are trying hard to understand the paintings, Iris. But—'

Aunt Ursula's face went very still.

'But what?' asked Iris.

Aunt Ursula began to snore lightly.

Much later, they stopped on the outskirts of Sant Joan, at a petrol station. Aunt Ursula was still fast asleep with a slack mouth.

Señor Garcia turned the car off and peered through the windscreen, trying to catch the attendant's attention. When no one came, he got out of the car and began to fill the tank himself.

Iris followed him out. 'I need to use the bathroom,' she said.

Señor Garcia pulled a note from his wallet for the petrol. The station attendant stared through the window.

Iris took the note and trudged into the shop. There were shelves of chips and chocolate inside, bottles of oil and magazine racks. It was the same as the petrol stations at home, only the signs were in Spanish.

The attendant watched Iris all the way to the restroom doors, hissing through his teeth. He was still staring when she emerged again.

Señor Garcia had finished filling the tank and was now squeegeeing the windows. Another car pulled up on the opposite side of the pump.

Iris paid the attendant as quickly as she could. As she left, she glanced up at the circular mirror near the automatic doors. It was supposed to catch shoplifters, but instead Iris saw the attendant's reflection. He was making the sign of the cross, from forehead to chest and across to each shoulder.

When Señor Garcia swung the car in front of the house, a spectral Elna was there to greet them, holding a flickering candle in a jar. She wore a pink velvet tracksuit, but her face was made up as if she was headed to a nightclub. Her usual gold cross hung around her neck.

'Electricity gone. Maybe a tree fallen down,' she said, as Señor Garcia and Iris climbed out of the car.

The wind was whipping up anything in its path. A plastic plant pot clattered across the verandah, and the surrounding trees made sounds like crashing waves.

Leaning against Elna's legs was a fold-up wheelchair. She dragged it to the car door.

'This always happen when she go outside. I'm not a nurse, you know.'

Elna began to help Aunt Ursula into the chair. Iris was shocked to see how pale and weak her great-aunt was after their day trip.

'Iris!' Aunt Ursula called out in a whispery voice.

Iris leant around the car door.

'Once I saw an infinity of doors in the house. Doors that opened onto doors that opened onto doors—impossible to see where they ended. I've searched for years, but they're no longer in the same place. Do tell me if you come across them, won't you, Iris?'

'Yes, Aunt Ursula. Of course I will.'

'We've got it, Iris. Go inside,' ordered Elna.

Señor Garcia shooed Iris off with his white-gloved hands. It had turned into a freezing night, so Iris ran up the front stairs.

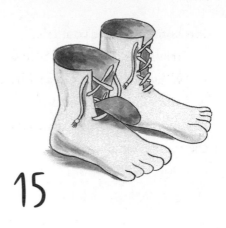

15

It was late when Iris woke to the sensation of steel jaws on her foot. For months she'd been getting cramps in her legs at night. *Growing pains*, apparently, which was rubbish. Growing up shouldn't hurt this much.

Iris pulled on her toes until the cramp eased. She tried the bedside lamp—the power was back on. Outside, the wind had eased.

Iris observed the foggy night through the guestroom window. The mountains were fuzzy and the box hedges around the garden were like castle walls. There was a golden flicker at the heart of the garden. Someone was down there.

Iris slipped on her sneakers and added a hoodie over her pyjamas. Señor Garcia had given her a torch because of the blackout, but it cast a feeble light.

Iris emerged onto the balcony. Sleepily, she walked up to the gold-and-velvet barricade that kept the east wing separate. *The mysterious east wing.* The black beyond was so dense it was almost solid. The darkness pulled on her but then something rustled loudly behind her.

'Dog, is that you?'

Even as she said it, Iris knew it wasn't the shadowhound. *Was it something downstairs?*

She faltered at the top of the stairs, prey to the same slithery feeling she'd encountered on her first day at *Bosque de Nubes*. Another rustle. The carpet on the staircase re-arranged its pattern. Leaves and flowers transformed into gold skulls against the red background.

Iris's breath snagged.

It's just the magic, she told herself. She started down the staircase. *It means you no harm, it's just doing its thing.*

A whisper laced the still air. A harder sound rose up. Iris glanced over the handrail and saw the tiles of the lobby move about like Scrabble pieces. They slid past each other until they formed letters:

I. R. I. S.

The tiles kept changing place—adding a D and an A—but Iris wasn't waiting. She was filled with the same inexplicable fear as when she'd seen, or thought she'd seen, the sketch of her own face in Uncle James's studio.

She ran down the remaining stairs and across the lobby.

The front door swung open and she ran through. Torch-light saw her down the side of the house, and past the birdbath and veggie patch.

The grassy slope at the rear of the house flashed under her feet. After she'd run through a gap in the hedge, she stopped.

A fire burned at the centre of the ornamental garden, at the foot of the horned statue. People were gathered around it, silhouettes wrapped in flames and smoke.

Someone in a black hood spoke and the group turned to look at Iris. A shape broke off and crunched across the gravel. Iris froze.

'It's little Eeris! Eeris!'

Elna tottered towards her in tight jeans and a duffel coat, her hair pulled into a high ponytail, long silver strands dangling from her ears.

'Shhhh!' she said, even though she was the one being loud.

The maid gave Iris a fierce one-handed hug that smushed Iris's face into her coat. In her other hand, Elna clasped a bottle in a brown paper bag.

'Little Australian, come,' she ordered.

Iris was dragged to the bonfire, which was set up in a rusted 44-gallon drum. She wanted nothing more than to go upstairs to bed, but Elna was determined for her to meet her friends.

Alex and Xavi lounged at the foot of the statue, sharing

a cigarette. They weren't that interested in Iris, and she didn't blame them.

Sophia, freckle-faced and chubby, warmed her hands at the fire. She lurched towards Iris, saying something in Spanish and then bossing Elna into translating.

'She say: *So really cute.*' Elna swigged from her bottle. Her cheeks were flushed and she kept looking sideways at Alex. 'Light off!' She slapped Iris's torch. 'It is secret, Señorita Freer not to know. Señor Garcia not to know.'

'What are you doing out here?' Iris asked.

Alex whispered in Xavi's ear and both men snickered. Iris had an awful premonition: this is what the girls at school would want to do soon, drink in the dark with boys who were more interested in talking to each other. Violet had already started hanging around the bus stop longer after school, trying to get the attention of the boys walking past.

'Party!' Sophia said suddenly in English, surprising even herself.

'We are having weather party,' Elna waved her hand. 'There is maybe clouds in the forest tonight, the mists.'

'Party,' Sophia said, quieter this time. She stared intently into the bonfire.

'Really there is no mist tonight, it is only a dud.' Elna looked morose. 'But what are you doing here, Eeris?'

'I couldn't sleep.' Iris felt small. 'I had a cramp.'

'I don't mean tonight, I mean *here,* in the house of the witch.'

The group grew quiet and looked at Iris.

'What witch?' A chill had spread through her body.

'Señorita Freer, of course. She who is never older, never die. Here, where there is not God.'

Elna talked to the sky. Her English had gone wonky, along with her sense of balance.

'Things that should not happen and why? Spells! Spells is why.'

'I hear she take the power from the young and give to herself, the old.' Alex stood up and straightened his jacket. 'I speak good English,' he said to the others, who were dumbstruck. 'Like a *vampir*, she take the power, the energies, from children to keep herself beautiful. My mother tell story of woman who do this and stay alive hundred of years.'

'Why I start work when I am in high school?' Elna seized control once more. 'Because it is good to have young person here! You can see tomorrow how she is—miracle!—so young and energy again.'

Elna drank from her bottle again. 'That is why are you here, Eeris.' She reeled, almost dancing in the firelight. 'You are wood for the fire!'

As if on cue the bonfire sparked upwards. Alex sat down again. Sophia's mouth hung open in a stupid way.

Iris filled with the impulse to charge Elna and push her over.

Why was she being so mean?

A sob worked its way up from her gut. She'd finally been getting on better with Aunt Ursula, which had been a relief when her parents had been so indifferent.

She turned and ran before the sob escaped.

It was very early the next morning when tapping woke Iris. She pulled a pillow over her head, but the tapping continued.

Iris dragged herself to the window and saw Jordi below, throwing a handful of gravel at her window, bit by tiny bit.

He mimed that he was waiting for Iris in the stables. Iris signalled that she would be down in ten minutes.

As she showered, Iris thought about the bonfire and how it had made everything spookier than it really was.

Aunt Ursula doesn't keep young people around her to steal their youth, she thought. *Nothing happened to Mum all those years ago.*

Everything felt different in daylight. She'd been an idiot to let Elna and her dumb friends upset her over nothing.

The east wing was still dark. The carpet had its usual leafy pattern and the floor tiles were abstract once more. Iris was about to go downstairs when she noticed something out of place on the opposite side of the balcony. It was almost as if someone had laid a mattress out to air, only the mattress was red, marbled with white and in the shape of a—

'Steak.'

Iris put a hand over her nose and mouth. There was a raw steak the size of a mattress draped over the railing. The giant piece of meat oozed liquid onto the carpet and smelt terrible.

Iris hoped Aunt Ursula would make Elna clean up the mess. It would serve her right.

Both Turrón and Miró stood at the front of the stable, saddled and waiting. Jordi waited nearby, a spare helmet in his hand.

'No way,' said Iris.

'Hear me out.'

Iris regretted teaching Jordi that particular expression. He was a sponge when it came to English—anything Iris said would pop out of Jordi's mouth the next day.

'There won't be any hearing you out. I'm not getting on one of those things.'

Turrón threw her a wild, contemptuous glance that Jordi did not notice.

'You want to find the eyeball tree, yes? My father says he has seen it once, and tell me where. But it is too far to walk. Better to ride.'

'Why aren't you at school, anyway? It's Tuesday, you should be there. Don't come crying to me if you…fail your Maths test and your dad gets mad.'

'My father says it is okay, because I have a new friend at *Bosque de Nubes*.'

'Cheating!' Iris said. Now she felt even more guilty, if that was possible. 'Don't say nice things. You won't convince me.'

'Don't you want to see the eyeball tree?'

Turrón high-stepped impatiently and Iris flinched.

'I swear on my new football that you will be safe.'

Iris felt crappy.

'It's not the eyeball tree, Jordi,' she admitted. 'The tree is just a clue. When I was looking at the real painting yesterday in Barcelona, what I was really looking for was the tiger. That's what I've been looking for all along. And I think the tiger could be near the eyeball tree.'

'*Un tigre?*' Jordi's whole body went slack with wonder.

'Yeah. A tiger. I realise it's not in the picture, but it's in the title, and Uncle James called it that for a reason. The paintings don't match up exactly with real life, so there's no reason why there isn't a tiger out there somewhere in the forest—I can feel it's true—and Aunt Ursula is always saying that my opinions about art are what's important, so—'

Iris stopped because Jordi was flapping his hands so hard she feared he would soon take off.

'Iris! Iris! *Dios mio...* Last night we come out to the stables because the horses are so, so *afraid* of something. They are walking up, down, and making noise, being on two legs. Papa look behind the stable and he find some poop...big poop.'

Jordi's accent when he said *poop* was nothing short of

hilarious, but Iris barely paid it attention. She was glad he hadn't questioned why she was so obsessed with the tiger.

'It's not fox poop, or horse poop, so what is it? Come on, Iris, what is it?'

'It was the tiger,' she said.

'Yes!' Jordi slapped his hands together. 'This is so dangerous!'

'No, it's not.' Iris started laughing about the poop, even as she was trying to be serious. 'We're only looking, right? Like in a safari, where you watch from a distance. That's not dangerous at all.'

Jordi would not be deterred. 'We will have to travel deep into the forest. On recon. Like in *Maximum Mission: Countdown* when Da Silva and his twin brother cross the Alps to look for the bomb factory?'

Iris sighed.

16

Marcel had stumbled across the eyeball tree—once, five years ago—near the bridge on the old dirt road that used to be the only way into Sant Joan.

Iris and Jordi picked up the village trail behind the cottage. Iris was concentrating hard so she wouldn't slide off Turrón. She'd never ridden a horse before and it was terrifying.

Jordi, on the other hand, was so comfortable on Miró he could have been drinking a cup of tea up there.

'Loose hands,' he said. 'Grip with your knees. And do this.'

Jordi leant forward and patted Miró's neck, but there was no way Iris could do that. Not only was she worried about falling off and being kicked by the horses, she was also terrified the horses might start talking or tap-dancing any moment now.

Anything's possible at Bosque de Nubes.

They took the path through light scrub, with the real forest way off in the distance. Iris gradually learnt to use her knees and sit up straight.

'So, you really think the tiger is near the eyeball tree?' asked Jordi.

'Maybe.' Iris was no longer really sure. The supposed droppings behind the stable had thrown her. 'I don't know. The eyeball tree is one of the easiest things in the painting to recognise, so I thought it would be a good place to start. I don't have many other good ideas.'

The day was so bright, the sky so clear and blue, that Iris forgot the dim events of the night before, and the difficulty of their search.

Jordi tried to teach her a song about an elephant and a spider as they rode, but she couldn't say the Spanish words nearly fast enough.

'What's that?'

Iris pointed at the ruin to their right.

'The old house.'

The building was ancient and crumbling. Jordi explained it had been built long before the main house. The house had dirt floors and the garden had crept inside—there wasn't any glass left in the windows, or doors, to stop it. Inside, the rooms lined the edges of a courtyard. A gnarled tree grew in the centre, its branches making a lacy green ceiling.

It's Aunt Ursula's dream, Iris realised. *Everything grown over and returned to nature.*

Iris crouched to look at an elaborate sculpture of a turtle's head, poking out from the wall. The turtle's mouth gushed a stream of water that disappeared mid-air. The ground was dry underneath.

'Iris!'

Jordi had found a white cross spray-painted on a window-sill. There were other markings nearby: squiggles, circles and numbers.

'I think the developers have been here,' Iris said. 'They're marking the building, for demolition probably. Knocking the house down, I mean.'

'This is not right.' Jordi's brow furrowed. 'They think they can own everything.'

Iris had to agree. She hadn't seen Jordi since running into Zeke Dangercroft in town, so she filled him in on what she'd learnt. Jordi was so furious Iris had to talk him out of going around to the Dangercrofts right then and there to grill him.

Iris knew how Jordi felt. Even when they were back on the horses, she couldn't help imagining what would happen to *Bosque de Nubes* if the developers took over.

How could the magic survive in the middle of a theme park?

It would be like a slow leak on a bicycle tyre—with the magic spilling out until nothing was left.

Iris had never seen a bridge so old before. Jordi called it an 'aqueduct' and said that it dated to the Roman Empire.

The towering bridge—two levels of elegant arches stacked on top of each other—spanned a whole valley, in a thin wedge of public land between part of the Freer and Dangercroft properties. It was so solid and perfect it was difficult to imagine it had stood there since Roman times. Iris wondered if her awe was what her dad felt about buildings and bridges. He never really talked that way about his work so it was hard to say.

Jordi tied Turrón and Miró securely to a tree. They were high on the east side of the valley, following a path that Jordi said was used by religious pilgrims in certain seasons.

Jordi led them down the dusty, gravelly slope to where the crossing began. There was a narrow notch built into the top of the bridge that ran all the way to the other side. Iris wasn't a fan of heights, but the edges of the bridge came almost up to her armpits—it would be impossible to fall off.

They walked along the sunken channel until they reached the middle and looked out over the valley. By now they were at least thirty metres up in the air.

'Good place of tiger watching,' commented Jordi.

He jumped up and leant over the barrier, a move that

made Iris feel queasy with nerves.

'Get down, Jordi!'

Iris scanned the different greens of the valley and sighed. It was weird that Marcel had seen the eyeball tree beyond the estate's boundaries. They had no chance of finding an eyeball tree here, or spying a small tiger slinking through the trees.

'Look.'

Jordi pointed at the red car parked at the entrance to the valley. It was well camouflaged under a stand of trees.

'Will they be putting crosses on *el acueducto*? Ruin something that has been here for two thousand years?'

Iris observed the two surveyors perched high on the valley wall, right up the other end. They were struggling to drag their equipment over the steep incline. The man was particularly agitated, looking around as if afraid they would be noticed. The woman took lots of photos.

Iris felt Jordi's resentment. A half-formed idea came to her.

'Jordi. There's a lot of mud and dirt and leaves and stuff down there, isn't there? And the surveyors are so far from their car...'

'You're right.' A grin spread slowly over Jordi's face. He raised his fist into the air. 'Protest! Revolution!'

'You sound like Aunt Ursula. It's scary.'

Together they walked back to the near end of the bridge, then made their way down to the lowest part of the valley.

On this side there were concrete steps built into the slope, with a metal handrail. Iris kept her eye on the surveyors. They were far away now. The man took measurements with the tripod thing; the woman talked on her mobile, gesticulating wildly.

Once at the bottom they ran from shrub to shrub, keeping low. Jordi began to bubble over with laughter.

'Shh!' Iris grabbed his arm and dragged him to the car. 'Be serious or we'll get caught!'

But she, too, could not help laughing as they grabbed handfuls of mud from the nearby slick and smeared it all over the windscreen.

There were envelopes and brochures and maps on the back seat of the surveyors' car, lying in a messy pile. Iris couldn't see them clearly enough to make out anything useful. Jordi checked the doors and the boot, but they were locked.

Iris's jeans were caked with mud, but she didn't care. She would never, ever have dared do this at home, but here it not only seemed right, it seemed necessary. It was people's homes at stake, and history—and magic too!

After the mud, they covered the car in leaves, pressing them into the muck. Jordi gave Iris two stripes of mud on each cheek and she did the same to him. Then they ran, breathless, up the stairs to where the horses were waiting for them.

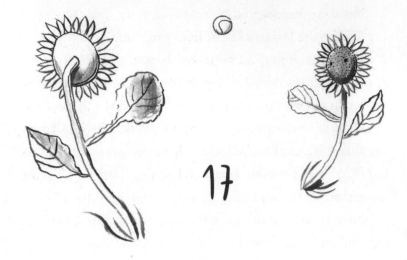

17

'On the way home there is one more place we look,' Jordi said.

Iris checked the paling sun, drawing ever closer to the treetops. She was parched and tired and her bum hurt from the hard saddle.

Jordi was paranoid that the surveyors would detect them if they took the highway, so they were back on the old village trail again, parallel to the main road. They passed over the fence line into Aunt Ursula's land.

'Don't you think it's too late? The light will be gone soon.'

They hadn't found a hint of a tiger or the eyeball tree. Jordi kept pointing to droppings or crushed bushes as evidence, but Iris knew he was just humouring her.

She was disappointed.

'There is at least one hour left,' Jordi said.

'But the tiger could be in the house or gardens,' Iris reasoned. 'It's not as if things here make sense, like tigers belong in forests…maybe the tiger will be in the bathroom.'

'That is a terror-frying idea,' Jordi replied. 'But I was thinking. To make a painting there are many things to carry. You must visit again and again. But the trees in the painting are very old. So we should look for a place that is not far, with easy path, plus old trees. I think of somewhere.'

'I suppose that's sensible,' Iris said. Jordi had told her that he got terrible marks at school, but there was no doubting that he was smart.

The horses picked their way across a rocky stream that was hardly more than a trickle. Iris hugged Turrón as he lurched over, following Miró's swishing tail. She'd lost her bearings completely, and could only hope they were travelling towards the mansion. Once more, she was staggered by the size of the Freer estate. If she'd been on foot she would have picked up a handful of stones to leave behind, Hansel-and-Gretel style.

'You won't leave me, will you, Turrón?' Iris patted the horse's neck. They'd bonded now.

Finally Jordi pointed out another trail through the ground ferns. After a few minutes they broke into a dim glade. This part of the forest was brown and peaceful. The ferns had given way to a carpet of russet leaves. The shallow basin was more than pretty enough to be the setting for a painting.

Down the middle of the clearing was a long narrow pond, flanked by an avenue of trees. After draping the horses' reins over a birch tree, Jordi took Iris on foot to where the path forked into two.

'I take this way, you take that.'

Iris was pretty sure the first rule of adventure was 'Don't split up'.

'We can see each other, all the time,' Jordi insisted.

Iris slapped at the mosquito feasting on her arm. 'Sure. But no wandering off—promise?'

'I promise! Call if you see anything.'

'Oh, don't worry, you'll hear me scream,' muttered Iris as she took the path downhill. She could see Jordi walking on the parallel path, a slight shadow moving in and out of the trees.

There was comfort in the fact that the glade wasn't completely wild. Someone had planted the avenue and built the pond. The pine needles were soft underfoot. Once or twice Iris thought she saw something in the corner of her eye, but it always turned out to be a weirdly shaped tree, or one of the dozens of red-winged birds that lived on the estate.

When Iris stepped over a raised tree root her gaze snagged on an unexpected object. In her distraction she didn't notice the figure darting up the slope to her right.

The stone slab poked up from the dead leaves. The words chiselled into it were dark against a coating of bright green moss.

IN MEMORY OF
BELOVED BROTHER
JAMES THOMAS FREER
28TH JUNE 1910—2ND NOVEMBER 1990

Iris stepped to the right, so she wasn't standing on top of Uncle James's grave.

It's a long way from the house—a strange place to bury him.

A few steps along was another headstone, this one smaller, older and almost collapsed into the earth. Iris pulled on the vine covering it. She whispered the epitaph out loud.

'*In loving memory of Iris Freer, who suddenly departed this life the 31st day of May, 1961, aged 41.*'

Iris shivered. *Forty-one is not that old. Mum is forty-three and Dad is forty-seven.*

Iris was so absorbed that she didn't hear Jordi's whistle.

'Eh! What you looking at, Iris?'

Jordi was a blob on the other side of the clearing. Iris moved to the right to see him better. There was a shape moving behind him through the trees.

'Jordi! Behind you!'

Iris yelled as loud as she could. It was hard to see if *the thing* was moving on all fours, or two legs.

But Jordi misunderstood and waved.

Iris shouted the word she'd only ever said twice in her life and ran.

Across the glade, jarring her knees on the uneven ground. Through the mud and the line of cherry trees. There was no time to go around the pond, so Iris jumped it. Turrón and Miró both reared into the air, hooves madly pedalling.

'Behind you! Behind you!' Iris screamed as she reached him.

Jordi finally got the idea and sprang into action.

'It goes for the road!' he yelled back.

Together they ran to the top of the hill and beyond, crashing through the undergrowth. The horses pounded near them with a whinny, then away.

Iris had never run so fast, for so long. By the time they'd reached the driveway, they were both gasping. The driveway was empty.

A thin, beaded scratch ran across Jordi's cheek. 'The tiger?' he wheezed.

'I have no idea.' Iris tried to catch her breath. The sun had dipped below the trees, bringing a chill to the air. 'I didn't see it properly.'

Jordi walked in circles, puffing. '*Dios mio*, the horses.'

'Where will they go?'

Iris pictured Turrón and Miró jumping the fence and galloping along the highway to Sant Joan.

'If we are lucky, they run to the stable. If we are not lucky, then Papa—' Jordi mimed having his throat slit.

Iris retied her shoelaces and they slowly walked back. Jordi believed more in her tiger sighting than she did.

'We have evidence,' he said. 'And we must keep hunting. Perhaps I will be sick from school all week.'

'Your dad will never agree to that. Especially now that we've lost his horses.'

'They will come home. Eventually.'

Iris remembered the date on Uncle James's lonely gravestone and realised that she would leave Spain on 2nd November, the anniversary of his death. It wasn't a good omen.

'I leave so soon,' she said. 'We won't find the tiger in time.'

'You will come back. Señorita Freer will give the house to you, for when she die.'

'What makes you say that?'

Iris kicked a rock. The fountain and the roundabout were visible in the distance.

'Papa thinks you can be the new owner of *Bosque de Nubes* and then you would never let anyone touch it.'

'Aunt Ursula isn't going to die soon. She's not that old.'

'She was already old lady when my parents move here.' Jordi stopped and twitched. 'Iris…' he squeaked.

Iris didn't see it at first. The road was empty, but a dark shape skulked near the left edge, 100 metres in the distance.

The tiger.

A spark of electricity ran down Iris's spine and set her feet in motion. She sprinted towards the animal.

This isn't going to be like the Loch Ness monster, she resolved. *I'm going to see this thing properly.*

Her sneakers slapped against the road. The tiger hadn't spied her yet, but she saw it leaving the safety of the trees.

Iris was twenty metres away when she realised that everything about the tiger was wrong. It walked on two legs. It had no tail, or stripes. It was dark brown, not yellow.

As if sensing her confusion, the creature turned and stared. Iris's legs failed as quickly as they'd first made themselves useful. She slammed to a halt.

She was now close enough to see brown tufts of fur and opalescent scales. Eight arms waved from its sides in a confusing tangle.

The creature wasn't a stranger—she and Jordi had created it. Bear's head, spider's body, reptilian legs, high-tech running shoes. Only it wasn't texta and paper, it was real. Three-dimensional, flesh and blood, real.

The creature fixed on Iris calmly with its yellow eyes and snorted. One thin spider arm unfurled from the many and hovered through the air towards her.

Iris stepped back. The limb ended in a fine curved hook.

The creature retracted its arm and loped out of the way on its serpentine legs, fast and sure, into the forest. Seconds later there was nothing to show it had been there.

Iris stopped holding her breath.

Jordi was kneeling where she'd left him, with his hands clasped in front of his chest. When he saw Iris looking, he got to his feet and jogged towards her.

'Did you see that? Did you see that?'

Iris grabbed onto Jordi when he reached her. Her lungs were going to burst right through her rib cage.

Jordi's knees were dirty and the whites of his eyes were showing. After a confused pause he started laughing so hard that, within seconds, he was almost as out of breath as Iris.

'We made it. We made that animal!' chanted Iris. 'Be serious, Jordi, please! *Gracias!*'

'Sorry, sorry.' Jordi wiped his eyes. 'It was not a tiger.'

'Exquisite Corpse,' said Iris, with all the energy she had left.

Beyond the dining room where the dinner party had been held was the corridor that led to Aunt Ursula's bedroom. Iris hastened that way, carrying her Exquisite Corpse drawing.

The walls were painted cream to match the carpet in this part of the house, creating a snowstorm effect. Light showed through an open door at the end of the corridor.

'Aunt Ursula?'

Iris collided with Elna at the bedroom door. The maid had her usual headphones around her neck, a tinny *boom-boom-boom* blasting from them. She had a hairdryer in her hands.

Iris frowned.

'Señorita Freer must rest.' Elna was as blunt as ever. 'No can disturb. She's very tired still.'

A voice came from inside. 'Stop fussing, Elna, and let her in. Take the hairdryer to Reynaldo, he'll know what to do.'

Elna screwed her mouth up.

'Do you have something to say to me, Iris?'

'No.' Iris frowned even harder and shuffled her feet.

'Oh.' Elna tilted her head. She had dark circles under her eyes. 'Because I think you like to tell me how much I am an idiot. An idiot who drink too much and says many stupid things?'

'Maybe...' said Iris.

'I thought so, little Australian.' Elna picked up Iris's hand to check her polish. 'Still no chip, *muy bien,*' she said with approval. 'I owe you another manicure now, for apology. Anything you want. You want real diamonds? Zigzag? No problem.'

She pointed the hairdryer at Iris then slunk down the hallway.

Aunt Ursula's bedroom was lit by the buttery glow of

a lamp. The wallpaper was cream striped with gold. Aunt Ursula sat on an old-fashioned four-poster bed with a newspaper by her side. She removed her reading glasses.

'Are you sick?' Iris asked.

Aunt Ursula looked tiny on the grand bed and was ghostly pale. She peered at Iris.

'Perhaps I should be asking you the same thing?'

Iris remembered that she was covered in mud and probably had leaves in her hair. She hurried to her great-aunt's side.

'It came to life! The picture—it came true!'

Aunt Ursula's whole body tensed. 'Whatever do you mean?'

'What Jordi and I drew! It came to life!' Iris held out the picture frame. 'It's real. Part-bear and part-spider, part-lizard too, on the driveway. I chased it, but it got away.'

'Ohhh…' Aunt Ursula seemed relieved.

Iris tried to untangle her words.

'The Exquisite Corpse, Aunt Ursula. It's a real living and breathing animal, out there in the forest. I have no idea how it happened, but we drew it—and it came to life!'

Aunt Ursula finally spoke. 'So, it wasn't a moving drawing, as in an animation…and it wasn't an apparition?'

'No, it had fur like a real bear. And when I got closer it smelt of wet jumpers.'

Iris took the frame from Aunt Ursula.

'I thought Uncle James painted what he saw here, at the

estate. I figured that was how it worked. But this means it can also work the other way—draw something and *then* it becomes real.'

Aunt Ursula blinked once, twice, three times. A strange atmosphere hung in the air.

'Are you all right?'

Aunt Ursula snapped into focus. 'I apologise, Iris. I'm very excited, I only wish I could have observed it myself. Tell me, is it a friendly creature?'

Iris pictured the creature's clear gaze, and the springy, natural way it moved.

'Yes, I think so.'

'And healthy?' Aunt Ursula enquired.

'I suppose. Maybe we could do an Exquisite Corpse drawing together and see if it comes to life too?'

Aunt Ursula crossed one hand over the other. 'And what if, next time, the creature is neither healthy nor friendly?'

Iris dwelt on that for a moment. 'You know, in books when people use magic, there's always a price. Like, if they get something good through magic, then something bad happens as well.'

Aunt Ursula was silent for so long Iris felt embarrassed.

'But that's just in books, it doesn't mean real life,' she added.

Aunt Ursula patted Iris's hand. 'You make a good point. Balance is important.'

'Can I help you with anything around the house?' Iris

offered. Not because her mum had instructed her to do so, but because her great-aunt still seemed so distracted and unwell. The trip to Barcelona had really drained her.

'There is something, actually. Reynaldo has an errand to run tomorrow morning—would you be able to go with him? He has to take a delivery to the Dangercrofts' house, but if he goes alone that Shirley woman will eat him alive. Or talk him to death.'

Iris didn't let on that she knew anything about what needed to be delivered. 'Of course,' she said. 'You can count on me.'

18

The Dangercroft mansion was a cartoon palace. A Frankenstein's monster of several different historical periods, with extra cherubs, flagpoles and turrets.

Or, as Dad would probably say, thought Iris, *too much money and not enough taste*. She couldn't help wishing she *hadn't* asked Aunt Ursula if she needed help with anything.

Señor Garcia was even more flustered than usual, so Iris tried to take charge as best she could.

The Dangercrofts' doorknocker was in the shape of a rose. Señor Garcia struggled to lift the package from the boot.

'Oh, hi,' said Iris, when the door was unexpectedly opened by a teenage girl with pale-blue hair. 'Is Mrs Dangercroft here? We've got an, um, delivery.'

The girl leant forwards. A silver ring through the middle part of her nose glinted. 'If you value your life,' she whispered, 'do not eat anything cooked by my mother.'

'Hellooooo!' Shirley Dangercroft pushed the girl aside. 'Oh, it's the Australian! You've brought my painting!'

'She didn't sleep at all last night.' The girl smirked. 'She's always wanted to own a painting by a dude she knows nothing about—except that his paintings are worth *squillions*.'

Iris's mouth twitched. The girl smiled lazily.

'Iris, this is my daughter, Willow.'

Shirley peered behind Iris. Her hair was redder and bouncier than ever.

'MISTER GARCIA,' she hollered. 'Please, both of you, welcome to my humble abode.'

The Dangercrofts' abode was not humble: the entrance hall was the size of a football field. Their sweeping staircase made a joke out of the staircase at *Bosque de Nubes*.

Iris helped Señor Garcia carry the sheet-wrapped painting. The driver's face was pinched and nervous. Iris could still feel the faintest crackle of electricity from yesterday's chase in her arms and legs.

Shirley ushered them into a light-filled room with floor-to-ceiling windows, floor-to-ceiling curtains and floor-to-ceiling bookshelves. She swept aside the textbooks that were scattered across a large table.

'Excuse the mess. Our Willow is home schooled. She's

very gifted so there's no point her going to a normal school.'

Willow closed her laptop. It was pink with a skull and crossbones sticker on the lid.

'Can you see my enormous brain?' she asked Iris. 'I've heard it's visible from outer space.'

'It's definitely at least fifty per cent bigger than a regular Australian brain,' Iris replied and Willow smiled.

'Where will we do this?' Shirley shrieked. 'I Am All A-Tizz! What about over here?'

She indicated the overstuffed leather couches in the centre.

'MISTER GARCIA, BRING THE MASTERPIECE OVER HERE FOR THE UNVEILING.'

Iris gave Señor Garcia a sympathetic look. Shirley was under the impression that because he didn't talk, he couldn't hear very well either.

Iris helped him position the painting on the couch. She was curious to see which painting Aunt Ursula had been willing to let go.

'Shouldn't Dad be here for this?' Willow asked. 'Seeing how it's his money that bought it and all.'

'Oh, please, Willow. I'm independently wealthy.' Shirley puffed her hair. 'I'm no trophy wife. I stand on my own two feet,' she told Iris.

Señor Garcia slowly removed the wrapping from the painting. When he was done, Shirley clapped.

The painting portrayed the now familiar insect with

googly eyes and a dignified air. A long, curly black wig sat on its bald head; a froth of white lace circled its pencil-thin throat. A great length of maroon satin had been thrown over the insect's shoulder, falling to the floor in thick folds. It pointed a stockinged leg forwards and delicately held a wooden sceptre, as if it were a sewing needle.

'Whoa, Louis XIV,' said Willow. 'The Sun King.'

'Adorable!' declared Shirley. 'It is going to look a treat on our bedroom wall.'

'She doesn't get my historical references,' said Willow. 'My own family doesn't understand me.'

'Or maybe in the dining room,' continued Shirley, 'so when we have parties everyone can look at it. There are only thirteen Freers in private collections, worldwide.'

All Iris could think about was the box of costume items she'd seen Señor Garcia carry into the studio. It was too much of a coincidence—the wig, the silky red material—but in the full light from the windows, the oil paint was clearly faded and cracked. Perhaps if she got closer—

'No fingers on my painting!' trilled Shirley.

Señor Garcia was in a far corner, inspecting a table lamp with a rather handsome glass shade. When he saw Iris looking he straightened with a guilty expression.

'Marisol!' yelled Shirley Dangercroft. A French maid came running.

'Would you fancy a treat before you go, Iris?' Shirley ushered the maid forwards. 'I was so excited this morning—only baking could calm me down. It's a traditional Spanish recipe.'

The plate held a dozen bloated biscuits. They were studded with green and blue and yellow candy bits, and were far from traditional.

Willow appeared over her mother's shoulder, jabbing two fingers in her mouth. Iris had to think quickly.

'Thank you, Mrs Dangercroft, but I'm allergic to gluten.'

Willow gave Iris the silent thumbs-up.

'You're missing out.' Shirley bit into a biscuit. 'Tell me, Iris, where does your family come from? You're so exotic-looking.'

'Melbourne.'

'Oh no, that's not what I meant.' Shirley caught a piece of biscuit as it fell from her mouth. 'I mean, where is your family *from*?'

'Mother! Iris doesn't want to stand here all day, talking to us.'

'Actually, if you ever want to'—Iris was going say *play* but then realised how babyish it would sound—'hang out at *Bosque de Nubes* with me and Jordi, that's my friend, well...' She trailed off. Willow was too cool to spend time with them.

'Willow is very busy with her studies,' Shirley said, showing Iris and Señor Garcia to the front door. 'We're fast-tracking her so she can finish high school early.'

156

Shirley handed Iris an envelope. 'The rest of the asking price, sweetie. Give it to your great-aunt. Thanks so much. Toodle-ooo!'

'Come over anytime!' yelled Willow from the other room. 'Save me!'

19

Iris found Aunt Ursula sitting with Jordi on the patio, eating custard straight out of the oven pan. A striped umbrella shaded their table. Both were laughing fit to burst.

Turrón and Miró hung their heads over the stable doors, seemingly unharmed. Marcel was hand-feeding them carrots. Maybe Iris imagined it, but when Marcel saw her she was pretty sure he scowled. He was dressed oddly, in a silky green shirt and dark pants, with a red sash around his waist.

Iris hurried up the steps.

'When did they get back?' she asked. 'The horses?'

'During the night.' Jordi was dressed similarly to his father. 'We get up this morning and they are nosing in the garden, hungry for hay. Not even a scratch is on them.'

'How did you go at the Dangercrofts?' Aunt Ursula handed Iris a spoon. The custard had a layer of crackly brown toffee on top and was bright yellow underneath. 'A successful delivery?'

Iris handed over the envelope and perched on a spindly chair. An air of mirth still surrounded the table.

'What's so funny?'

'Young Jordi was just telling me about your prank with those nasty developers' car.'

Aunt Ursula's eyes were sparkly and her cheeks flushed. She'd finally bounced back from their Barcelona excursion. Even her skin was less wrinkled.

'A very inspired idea, Iris, I must say. There's nothing quite like a bit of grass roots activism. You should do whatever you can to get rid of them!'

'Right.' Iris wondered what else Jordi had told Aunt Ursula. *Would he be careless enough to mention the tiger?*

'Someone from the building company came to our school today.' Jordi stopped shovelling custard into his mouth for a second. 'They were saying the theme park is new and exciting and there will be lots of jobs, in building and in *turismo*.'

'I've never heard anything more foolish than an art-themed amusement park. You can't dish out art to people on a platter.' Aunt Ursula struck the oven pan with her spoon. 'And it's very underhand, going direct to the children. Hoping that they all go home to their parents and beg them for a roller-coaster.'

'Not me!' Jordi thumped himself on the chest. Iris had no idea why he was being such a suck.

'I know you wouldn't dream of it, young man.' Aunt Ursula dumped their spoons in the scraped-clean pan. 'Your moral compass is extremely steady.'

She took the dish into the kitchen, leaving Jordi and Iris alone on the patio. Iris ached with questions about the painting that Aunt Ursula had sold to the Dangercrofts, and wondered about her great-aunt's own *moral compass*.

'I did not understand any of the words Señorita Freer just use,' said Jordi.

'What else did you tell her?' Iris knew she sounded grumpy, but she couldn't be bothered hiding it. 'And why are you dressed like that?'

'It's for *Castillo*. It's a local thing we do, making human towers. Come with me, I don't want to talk here.'

Iris followed Jordi down the less frequented side of the house, where there was straggly grass, the whitewashed outside wall, and a freestanding arch that held up nothing and led nowhere.

'It was *our* secret that we trashed that car,' said Iris, but that wasn't what Jordi wanted to discuss.

'I have a really good plan. It's even better than what we done yesterday. We are going to *take matters into our own hands*.'

Iris crossed her arms. Aunt Ursula must have taught

Jordi that expression because she sure hadn't.

'I did not tell Señorita Freer all the informations. See? I can keep the best secrets. After the school talk I make conversation with an evil businessperson. And guess what? Go on, guess?'

'Just tell me.'

'I find out where they will be tomorrow! At the fake lake, the reservoir.' He stumbled over the word. 'Finding out about...something. I got bored listening. But what is important is that we will be there and we will scare them.'

'How?'

'The Beast Car!' Jordi waited for Iris's reaction. 'You remember? The car with feet? We make it go *loco*—so, so crazy—on the developers!'

'How are you going to do that?'

'Not really sure,' Jordi admitted. 'But first we make the car angry, you know, like the bullfighting in the stadium. We get it to the reservoir. Then maybe we put something in the fuel tank, like coffee or...or...sherry. Or we kick it in the bumper. We make it go fast—can you imagine? It scares them off.'

Iris barely knew how to reply.

'That is the stupidest idea I've ever heard. One, you have no idea if it's going to work because you haven't thought it out properly. Two, it sounds really dangerous. Three, have you thought what would happen if word got out about the magic? Things would be a billion times worse if they realised that they could make a real magical theme park!'

Jordi flamed red in the face. He looked startlingly similar to Marcel.

'I've seen it before, Iris! Even when people see the magics they don't believe it. So all they are going to see is a really scary car. After they don't remember why, but they think: this is a really bad place. And they stay away.'

'You can't be sure of that!'

'Señorita Freer says we should do whatever it takes! Do you want her to be kick from her home? Do you want me and Papa to have nowhere to live? During the civil war here we fight the *fascistas*, even secretly, because when we see a wrong thing we do something about it. That is what we are like. But maybe Australian is different.'

'It's a really stupid idea.'

'Oh, oh, *estúpido*? As stupid as a *tiger*?' Jordi faltered ever so slightly on the last word but kept his chin held high.

'What did you say?'

'My plan is not as stupid as the dream of a tiger.' Jordi spoke quietly now. 'I help you, Iris, with looking for the tiger and I don't even think it's the best idea. But I do it because I think we are friends now. And now, you won't help me.'

Jordi looked upset. His lower lip might have been trembling. But Iris couldn't back down.

'If you think my ideas are so dumb then I don't want

your help anymore. We can both do things on our own.'

And then she stomped off.

Iris scanned the ground floor for a missing painting, a blank spot where there should have been a frame. All the downstairs lights were blazing, keeping the night at bay, but the house felt deserted. Iris had shared a silent cup of tea in the kitchen with Señor Garcia, still shaky from the fight with Jordi, but now the driver was nowhere in sight.

There were no gaps on the walls. Iris had searched in all of the unlocked rooms.

It didn't matter. She was almost certain she'd never noticed Shirley's insect portrait anywhere in the house. The English ladies at the art gallery had said that lots had been found in an attic, so it was possible Aunt Ursula had pulled the painting out of a dusty room somewhere. But that didn't explain the costume Iris had seen in the green-house studio.

Iris went to Aunt Ursula's bedroom. There was a light on, but her great-aunt wasn't there. The alarm clock on her bedside table said it was half past nine—where would Ursula be so late?

Her satin pyjamas had been left out on the bed, perfectly smooth. On the bedside table were several crumpled pieces of paper, an eraser and a graphite pencil. Iris eased the papers out. The first was a sketch of Señor Garcia, in his driver's uniform and cap. It was strange, but the drawing somehow showed more detail to Señor Garcia's face than Iris had ever seen in real life.

The second drawing was of Iris. It was very similar to the drawing that she'd seen in the greenhouse studio but less complete. She had a face and eyes and a nose, but no mouth yet.

It was Ursula who drew me, it dawned on Iris. *Not Uncle James's ghost.*

She replaced the drawings and reversed out of the bedroom.

What am I missing? she thought. *What am I not getting? There's something big going on...*

The ornate lobby ceiling held no answers. Iris imagined the chandelier unmooring itself and crashing in a crystal symphony around her. She felt like the only person left on the planet.

In the far distance there was a rumble of thunder. Iris went upstairs.

When Iris woke after only a few hours' sleep it was not with a cramp. The lightshade looked like a UFO from this angle. A memory came to her.

It had been a few days before she'd left for Spain. Iris had gone to the study to talk to her dad. Her mum wanted him downstairs, and her dad sighed as if he didn't want to be interrupted. He slid his computer chair back from his big drafting desk.

But before that, before the chair sliding and the sighing, her dad had quickly rearranged his papers. He'd covered something up.

Iris kicked her feet, trying to loosen the bedsheets. Elna made the beds as if she'd been army-trained. There was something not quite right at the bottom of her bed. She wiggled her toes and felt smooth leather and rough stitching.

Iris sat bolt upright, threw off the covers, and there they were, *on her feet*, laced up and ready to go—the feet-boots.

'No way,' said Iris and, as if they'd been waiting for her, the feet-boots dragged to the floor.

'No no no no no!'

Iris only had time to grab her dressing-gown before the feet-boots sent her lurching for the door. She clung to the handle, but they kept marching until she had to let go, or have her arms ripped off.

All was dark on the first floor balcony. Iris squeezed her eyes shut. She only opened them again when she heard a chime; they'd collided with the post and rope barrier that shut off the east wing.

'Oh, great,' said Iris. 'Go right ahead. This is an awesome idea.'

The feet-boots did not do sarcasm. They squeezed past the barrier into the dark corridor. When Iris's vision adjusted, she saw faint suggestions of a high ceiling, patterned carpet and ghostly white doors.

'Where are you taking me?'

Her voice echoed. Iris had the weird feeling she'd lost her body and become part of the night.

She lurched down the corridor, trying not to think about the possibility of crashing through the rotten floor. The wood squeaked under her feet.

After a while she became aware of rectangles—pictures on the wall. There were dozens of them, one after the other. She leant towards the wall, glued safely to the floor by the boots. An oval, a cream curve, a dark slash. The paintings were similar and endless.

Iris leant further, and then the unthinkable happened—the world tilted right over. She threw her arms out, and they were suddenly above her head. The corridor spun; the ceiling became the floor and the floor became the ceiling.

When Iris opened her eyes she found herself in a narrow staircase, the feet-boots taking two stairs at once. At the top was a square of moonlight and air.

The night poured in, the starry sky swooped to meet them, and Iris was standing on the roof, gasping in the cold air. She knew it was the roof because there was nothing above her but a million stars.

The roof was flat and shaped in an H. A short wrought-iron fence circled it.

Iris stood on the middle bar of the H. The feet-boots shifted, taking a step towards the edge of the roof, then another.

'Oh no,' she said, already trying to crouch and tip herself over. 'Oh no, you don't.'

She burned with the effort of stilling her feet, but to no effect. The boots walked her all the way to the iron fence, the only thing between her and a twenty-metre plummet to the ground. She beat her palms against her head with frustration. Her tummy pressed against the fence and the boot toes scraped the edge of the roof.

The front garden lay below: the overgrown hedges, the patchy lawn and the roundabout. The marigolds around the fountain were bright orange against dark brown dirt.

The orange dots broke free from the crumbly soil, forming lines and then letters, just like the mosaic tiles of the lobby.

Iris leant out further as they arranged into the letters of her name *I R I S*, then a sketchy E R. She waited for the *T I G* to complete the message. But when the flowers settled, this is what they said:

I R I S   D A N G E R

Immediately, the leather boots slackened and Iris shuffled away from the roof edge. She removed the boots as quickly as she could and then hurled them off the roof, out into the night.

Iris took the stairs with wobbly legs and bare feet. She kept her hand on the wall while she made her way slowly back to the main part of the house. The hallway reeked of fresh paint.

She stuck her face close to each painting as she passed it: they were all of Aunt Ursula as a young woman. Her clothes changed, sometimes the way she sat changed; sometimes she wore a faint smile. Each was signed simply with the familiar initials *J.F.*

Iris traced the signature and felt tacky paint. She rubbed her fingertips together.

The painting was still wet.

20

There was no stopping Aunt Ursula entering the guestroom, even though Iris had used the god of thunder and lightning statue to barricade herself in.

'You have a visitor downstairs,' Aunt Ursula said.

Iris lowered the book of Spanish fairytales she'd found in the upstairs library. Fairytales were the same wherever you were in the world: princesses, princes, dying kings, evil stepmothers, kind and cruel fairies.

For a second, Iris assumed Aunt Ursula meant Willow Dangercroft, and her spirits lifted.

'If young Jordi doesn't pass his exams,' Aunt Ursula continued, 'I rather imagine it will be on your head. I'll be surprised if he goes to school at all this week.'

Iris raised the book again. 'Well, *I* imagine it's his own

business if he wags school.'

'Well said.' Aunt Ursula laughed, not feeling the frost in the atmosphere. 'He's waiting on the porch, but he won't come inside.'

'I don't want to speak to him.'

'Well, I don't have terribly much to do today if you wanted to help me in the vegetable garden. Or perhaps you're interested in playing cards?'

Iris grunted. She knew Jordi had come up with his stupid scheme himself, but she couldn't help thinking that Aunt Ursula was to blame with all her talk of activism and protest.

Aunt Ursula leant down to pat the statue on the head.

'I'm glad you've made friends with Apocatequil,' she said. 'He's a dear thing despite being a bit of a pest. He's pre-Columbian. That makes him a thousand years old. I bought him when I lived in Mexico. Had to bargain very hard, as a matter of fact.'

Aunt Ursula lingered in the doorway. Iris continued to pretend she was not there.

'When I had to leave Europe, I went to Mexico instead of returning to Australia. I was there almost eight years. There was quite a group of us living there after the Second World War. I could show you photos…?'

'Maybe.' Iris did not lift her gaze from the page. Eventually Aunt Ursula left.

Iris stared into the murky tunnel of the east wing, as if daring it to cough in her face. She couldn't get the paintings hidden there—so many of them in the darkness—out of her mind. She checked the old family photos in the sitting room again, and the painting of Iris Freer and the five-legged dog. The shadowhound hadn't shown itself for days. It seemed like a distant memory.

Jordi's right about the tiger, Iris realised, with queasy regret. *There's no evidence that it exists. Maybe I've been distracting myself and wasting time.*

In the ballroom, Iris recalled how Señor Garcia had walked to the end of the room and disappeared into thin air.

When Iris pressed against the skinny ballroom window she saw Señor Garcia below, for real, bent over the open bonnet of Aunt Ursula's cream-coloured car. It was the angelic version of the evil twin black car with feral feet.

Jordi hadn't read the newspaper article, so he didn't know that the car had crashed into a tree with Iris Freer inside. And Aunt Ursula had no idea what plan Jordi might come up with to thwart the developers because she hadn't seen the Beast Car.

Señor Garcia looked up and waved his spanner. Iris swallowed past the lump in her throat. She had to go after Jordi.

According to Señor Garcia's sign language, the reservoir was easy to find. You turned right onto the main highway and kept going for 500 metres. A service road on the right wound through trees until it hit the big body of water.

Señor Garcia wrote the word *EMBALSE* on the dusty car window. His hands were coated with grease.

The bike ride to the reservoir was bumpy and Jordi's seat was too low for Iris. She rode on the shoulder and kept an eye out for cars that drove on the wrong side of the road.

Iris's legs were powered by guilt and dread. *If I hadn't lost my temper, I could have persuaded Jordi instead of insulting him*, she realised. *I could have told him why he should avoid the Beast Car.*

She almost missed the white *0,8 EMBALSE* sign half covered in shrubbery. The reservoir road wound gently downhill through light forest.

At the bottom was a car park holding two white vans. A dirt road continued around the corner.

Iris laid Jordi's bike at the foot of a tree. The air was still, only interrupted by birdcalls and the distant hum of the highway.

The reservoir curved below, a lovely kidney-shaped lake. It was fringed with fir trees and fishing spots. At the far end was a huge concrete wall.

Iris couldn't see anyone around. She'd expected to stumble on a scene of devastation: people screaming, and Jordi run over, with claw marks across his middle. Perhaps she was too early, or perhaps Jordi's plan had failed from the start. Maybe the car couldn't travel beyond the borders of magical *Bosque de Nubes*.

The vans were identical, white with two logos on the side: a green wheel and a red dragon. The driver's cabs were littered with drink cans and chip packets.

Iris walked to the side of the road and discovered a curious object: a broomstick with a furry trapper hat taped crudely to the end. Iris stared. She'd just figured out that the broomstick was homemade car-bait when she heard a low buzz. It stopped, started, then got louder. A rough-edged chainsaw rumble broke the quiet, and the Beast Car hurtled into sight, galloping up the steep dirt road.

It coughed dirty exhaust fumes and scrabbled its clawed feet on the sharp turn. The rear passenger door swung open as the car shunted across the road then slammed shut. Someone was inside, sliding across the back seat with flailing arms.

'Jordi!'

He plastered himself to the back window, only to slip out of view when the Beast Car spun on Iris, its metal grille bared. The air filled with a fury of revving—and then a long screech as the car zoomed off.

Iris could barely see through her tears. Her nose ran and she didn't care. The furry broomstick balanced across the handlebars precariously.

Iris rode back towards *Bosque de Nubes*. There were

claw marks on the road but they disappeared at the highway. Her legs had nothing left in them, but she kept pushing until the iron cloud gates came into view.

She didn't have to wait too long for signs of the car. Two tracks cut through the grass, only a few hundred metres from the gates, near the old Sant Joan riding track. A horn blared, over and over again.

Iris threw Jordi's bike into a ditch and made her way towards the sound, carrying the broomstick like a magical talisman.

The car ricocheted through the clearing, ripping up the wildflowers. Great clouds of steam spewed from its bonnet. Iris stood on the edges, unsure.

Only when Iris saw Jordi wave at her frantically did she spur herself into action again. She held the broomstick out in front of her and advanced, slowly.

'*Hellooooo*, over here!'

She waved the broomstick through the air in what she hoped was a hypnotic fashion. The Beast Car flashed its cracked headlights.

Iris crept forwards. If the car revved she was going to run for her life.

'Look at me…what have I got?' she called in a singsong voice. 'Funny, furry stick!'

Miraculously, the car lowered itself onto the ground, splaying its hairy feet on each corner. There was a heavy thump when its underside hit the dirt. Jordi had managed to wind a window down.

The car coughed and buzzed again, but it was more of a purr now. Iris laid the broomstick in the grass at the bumper bar and backed away.

'Nice car, nice car.'

Jordi slid his head and shoulders out of the window.

The car rumbled, a monstrous growl that built to a sound similar to a 747 jet taking off. Iris ran to Jordi and pulled him out of the Beast Car, milliseconds before it reared up on two paws, exposing its metal underbelly.

Jordi and Iris flew backwards, slamming into the dirt and rolling. A shower of white paper fragments billowed around them.

'Owww!' Iris's cheek hit gravel. She crawled aside as the Beast Car crashed down, gouging the dirt. Jordi yelped.

The car squealed, shot smoke from its rear, and galloped off. Iris lay on her back, winded.

'Iris, are you okay?'

Iris crawled to Jordi. He was covered in dust and his T-shirt was torn. He lay in a bed of scattered white brochures.

'You were right and I was wrong,' he said. 'I owe you my most humble apologies.'

'Shut up. Are you okay? Are you hurt?' Iris wheezed. He had alarming welts on his stomach. 'Let me see those. Do they hurt?'

Jordi brushed her hands off. 'No, no, leave it, I'm fine. I

want to say I am sorry. You saved my life, Iris. You saved me.'

'Don't be silly. I'm the one who should be sorry.' Iris's heart thumped unevenly. She picked up one of the scattered brochures. 'What are these?'

On the front was an artist's impression of the theme park, nestled into the hills near Sant Joan. It was hard to tell which was the real photo and which bits were computer generated.

'I took them from the developers' van.' Jordi coughed and rubbed his side. 'I stuck a bunch down my shirt. It's evidence.'

There was Spanish text inside the brochure, a map, more drawings, even a person dressed up as the park mascot: a bizarre, bobbly figure with a lobster on its head.

On the back of the brochures were rows of business logos. Iris recognised the wheel and the dragon at the very top, they were identical to the symbols on the vans at the reservoir. The other logos underneath were smaller, and then, in the bottom right corner, was something that made Iris stop breathing altogether.

There was a *C* and an *A* and three arrows pointing diagonally up, towards the future. Her father's business: Chen Architects.

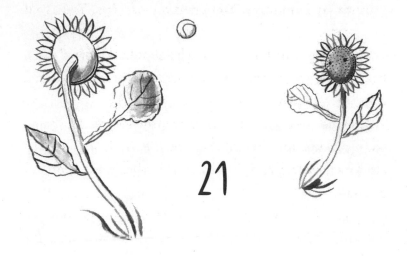

21

There was no hiding what had happened. Marcel spotted Iris and Jordi as they limped back to the main house, wheeling Jordi's bike between them.

After Marcel had ordered Jordi to the cottage, Iris slunk off as quickly as she could. She found herself retreating to the most unexpected place—the forgotten tennis court where all the madness had begun. The sunflowers were not in residence, so Iris had the court to herself.

She lay on the clammy grass and stared at the sky. The field of yellow grass was visible through the tatty wire fence; so were the tangled trees. The court suited her mood.

Her dad's firm was involved in the theme park. How, she wasn't sure. But if her dad was involved, then her mum was too. She would have convinced him to get involved in a big project with big money.

I'm one of those marionette puppets on a string, Iris thought. *I've been used. I thought I knew what I was involved in, but I don't.*

It didn't matter if Aunt Ursula held out against the developers, because her parents were looking to the future just like their logo. They wanted to destroy everything: magic, history and all.

Iris felt sick. Every friendship she'd made here had been built on lies. She paced up and down the fence, looking at the midnight tangle of forest.

How am I going to get out of helping my parents? And without Aunt Ursula or Jordi or Elna finding out what a traitor and fake I am?

A twig cracked sharply close by. Iris stilled herself.

There was light footfall in the dry leaves. Through the fence diamonds, Iris saw a thin figure dressed in plain dark clothes.

Señor Reynaldo Torres Garcia.

He wore his usual peaked cap but had added a grey trench coat over his navy uniform. He was carrying a familiar object: Jordi's broom handle with the fur hat taped to the end.

How did he get that? Iris stared. *I was sure we left it out in the forest.*

She moved quickly, trying not to lose sight of him. After circling behind the tennis court, she cut diagonally through the bracken.

Soon there were only twenty metres between them on the muddy track. There wasn't any time to worry about being taken deeper into the forest. Iris focused on Señor Garcia's bony shoulders. He had a peculiar way of walking: graceful and *un*graceful at once, like someone on stilts.

A camera flash went off in Iris's mind, or maybe it was a bolt of lightning.

Flash. Señor Garcia letting himself into the greenhouse studio, carrying props for his latest painting.

Flash. Never seeing him without a hat.

What if Uncle James had never died? Iris thought, with a quickening heart. *What if he'd kept painting all these years, painting endless portraits of his sister, and insect portraits when he and Aunt Ursula needed more money?*

The path rose and fell over a series of small hills. The silvery birch trees were evenly spaced, the ferns bright splotches of green. The Shakespeare play they'd studied at school came to Iris's mind.

Over hill, over dale
Through bush, through briar
Over park, over pale,
Through blood, through fire...

Iris climbed the next rise.

Señor Garcia had removed his trench coat and slung it over his arm. His steps quickened around the next corner.

When the path straightened, he was nowhere to be seen.

Iris stumbled into an outcrop of granite rocks shaped like marbles.

Where has he gone?

A fuzzy point of light hovered in the distance. It divided into two, then four. Soon there was a constellation of lemon-yellow lights bobbing in a large tree that rose among the rocks. A silhouetted Señor Garcia walked back and forth. Another light sprang up and Iris saw that he was lighting lanterns in the branches.

Señor Garcia removed his cap and placed it carefully on a rock. Iris could only see the back of his head. The driver took off his jacket next, then unbuttoned his shirt.

Uh-oh.

Iris whipped behind a hollowed-out tree. *What if Señor Garcia is a secret nudist? It explains why he's walked so far from home. Or is it Uncle James, removing his disguise?*

Iris splayed her fingers over her eyes. Naked people were fine in paintings and statues, but real life was another matter.

But the moment she saw Señor Garcia for who he really was, the fact that he *had* taken off all his clothes wasn't important at all.

He wasn't Uncle James in disguise.

Señor Garcia had a bald head, huge eyes and twiggy arms and legs. He clambered first over rocks, then easily up the tree, using the sticky nubs at the end of his six legs for suction.

Señor Garcia was a stick insect. A human-sized stick insect—the same one in Uncle James's paintings.

Iris crawled to the base of the tree. A collection of objects had been arranged at the foot, and in dark niches under the rocks: pine cones and pebbles, seashells and seed pods, cracked teapots, golf balls, bubble wrap tied in bows, a lampshade, a guitar with a broken neck, a fishing net and the fur-topped broom handle.

Above her, Señor Garcia was a mass of lines in the branches. More specks of light appeared, high above.

Iris was caught unawares when Señor Garcia the insect slid down the trunk and stood in front of her.

'Oh.' Iris had to remove her hand from her mouth to speak. 'I'm very sorry, Señor Garcia. Sir.'

She looked into his glistening black eyes. They took up half of his triangular head and were very beautiful, like bottomless pools of water.

Iris's brain struggled to keep up. *Is this really the person who's been driving me around all week?*

'I didn't mean to snoop,' Iris said, even though of course she had. She noticed Señor Garcia didn't have much of a mouth to speak with. It explained a lot.

'Nice tree,' she said, fidgeting. 'Your collection is amazing. The lanterns are…nice.'

Señor Garcia tilted his head and chirped. It was difficult

to tell what was going on behind those peepers.

He moved his four non-standing legs, waving them from side to side, until his whole body swayed. Just like in the ballroom, his lanky frame moved with surprising rhythm.

Señor Garcia closed his dark-water eyes and clicked. He appeared to be in a trance as he picked up a chalky rock and began to draw on the rock face.

He drew a face, a man's face, with wide-set eyes, a straight nose, thin lips and heavy eyebrows. He turned to Iris as his insect features changed. A mask tumbled over his brow, green shell transformed into pink flesh, and then he had his human face on—nose and eyebrows and all.

Iris gasped. Señor Garcia chirped.

He threw away the rock and grabbed another object from his pile of sacred objects. It was a framed photo of Ursula, a portrait from her younger days. Señor Garcia held the photo forward and unleashed a series of emphatic clicks and chirps.

He talked and talked, pointing to the photo, tilting his head from side to side. A wave of heat rose from Iris's ankles to her face. The more he chirped, the less she understood.

'Yes,' she said eventually, purely to make it stop. 'I know what you mean.'

Señor Garcia gestured that they should go. They retraced their steps to the house. Iris was glad for their silence. She wanted to cry. She remembered Ursula's dream of destruction and she couldn't help imagining bulldozers moving through the forest, knocking over Señor Garcia's precious tree.

22

Fortunately, it was Willow who opened the door to the Dangercroft mansion. She seemed happy to see Iris standing on the doorstep.

Iris was desperate to avoid everyone at *Bosque de Nubes*. On the walk to the Dangercrofts' house she hadn't been able to stop her mind racing.

My parents expect me to go along with whatever they do. They think I won't dare disagree with them about the theme park. Or maybe they'll keep lying to me, trying to keep it a secret. They must think I'm stupid. I have been stupid.

'This is the best thing that's happened all week, you've no idea,' Willow said in a low voice as she let Iris in. She'd added red tips to the ends of her blue hair. Iris couldn't think where she would have found hair dye in the middle of the Spanish countryside.

They weren't quiet enough. Shirley Dangercroft swept in on a cloud of perfume.

'Iris! What a delight!'

Iris mumbled hello while Willow pulled her towards the stairs.

'Iris has promised to catch me up on Australian history, Mom,' she said. 'It's a real weakness in my knowledge base. It might even be the difference between getting into college or not. We're going to go to my room to concentrate, yeah?'

Shirley pouted. 'Oh, honey, you've worked really hard this week. Don't you want to kick your heels up a bit?' She clapped with sudden inspiration, the jewels on her fingers sending speckles of light flying. 'We could have a girlie party—watch a rom com, paint our nails...'

She pressed a button on the wall. A giant movie screen began its descent from the ceiling of the next room.

'Maybe later, Mom...it's a great idea...'

'How about a sandwich? I'll have Marisol make you one. I've trained her to make real American-style heroes, Iris.'

'Do not look back, and above all do not show any fear,' Willow said as they took the marble and gold stairs. 'Dad is off playing golf and Mom is bored. She's been driving me nuts all morning.'

Iris trailed Willow through the upper floor of the palace and tried to keep her mouth from gaping at all the gold, crystal and marble. The carpet was about a foot thick; walking on it felt like walking on pillows.

'How long have you lived in Spain?' she asked.

'Just on three years now. Three *long* years. I still miss home.'

Willow took Iris left and then right. In her ripped black jeans and baggy black jumper, she looked like a ninja in the mostly pastel house.

They emerged onto another landing.

'And here we have the Roman-themed portion of the house,' Willow said. 'Or Mom's warped version of what ancient Rome might have been like.'

They paused to regard the replica Classical statues and the fake columns and the mural of an outdoor Roman bath.

'Hideous, isn't it? Mom's take on life is *more is more.*'

'Where did she put her new painting?'

'I'll show you.'

Willow led Iris into a bedroom that was the size of Iris's whole house in Australia. The portrait hung at the foot of a king-sized waterbed.

'So Mother can have sweet dreams about dashing insects,' Willow said.

Now she knew it was Señor Garcia, Iris looked at the painting with greater interest. She touched the canvas. It was dry, but did smell of fresh paint, and despite some cracking on the canvas, it was still too bright to have been painted over twenty years ago. Not that she was an expert, but she had looked at *a lot* of paintings in the last week.

Someone at Bosque de Nubes *is making these insect paintings*, she thought, *and it definitely isn't Uncle James's ghost.*

'I'd never admit this to Mom,' said Willow, 'but I actually like that twiggy little guy. Normally I hate her taste in art, but this one I could get used to.' She walked to the door. 'Let's go. Being in the olds' bedroom really creeps me out.'

Willow's room was unlike anything else in the house. In fact, it resembled a cave more than a bedroom, with dark purple walls and ceiling.

Willow had a loft bed with a desk underneath, a big bay window filled with cushions and a windowsill crowded with succulents and terrariums.

'Your bedroom is so cool,' Iris couldn't help saying.

Willow chucked a couple of beanbags on the floor. 'Glad you approve. Basically no one is allowed to come in here, so you're definitely a VIP.'

Stuck everywhere—to the walls, the bed, the windows, the vanity table—were drawings, pictures torn out of magazines and photographs. The underside of the loft was covered with dozens of hand-drawn comics.

'Did you do these?'

Iris walked closer. There was a comic about a private-investigator cat, and another one set in a high school ruled by teens who were secretly fairy folk.

'That's why no one can come in here,' Willow said from her beanbag. 'They'll realise that I've been drawing instead of studying.'

'Is this what you want to do? I mean, as a career?'

'That's what I'm hoping.'

'You should come to *Bosque de Nubes*, you'll love it there,' Iris blurted out. 'There's heaps more paintings to look at, and lots of things to draw...' She trailed off.

Aunt Ursula might not be pleased with a visitor, even if Willow's parents had been invited before. Willow would *see things*, for sure. She had all the imagination in the world, Iris could tell from her comics.

Iris sat down in the other beanbag.

'You just got the frowniest look on your face,' Willow remarked.

'I've got a lot on my mind.'

'Yeah, I hope you don't mind me saying this, Iris, but when I opened the front door, I did wonder what had happened to you. You look like the future of the planet is on your shoulders.'

Willow was right, Iris did feel that way, but she wasn't sure if she could confide in the older girl.

'I'm not sure where to start,' Iris murmured.

'Start anywhere. I'm a great listener.' Willow tugged on

the ends of her red-tipped hair.

'Well, first of all,' Iris began, slowly, 'what if you suspected that someone had sold a painting, saying it was one thing, when it was really another thing? Or might be.'

'Oh, Mom is rolling in money, Iris. Her family is old, old money, and she's happy with that bug, as am I. So it's irrelevant whether it's the real thing or not. *NEXT*.'

'Oh.' That had been easy. 'Okay. Umm, I had a fight with my friend Jordi. I said some really mean things to him and then I wasn't there when he needed me and he ended up in danger, and it was only luck that got him out of it. He thinks everything is fine with us now, but I don't think it is. I mean, I shouldn't have said those things in the first place.'

'All right.' Willow leant out of her beanbag to grab a purple highlighter from the desk. She began to colour in the ends of her hair, which was beginning to resemble a three-colours drink. 'First question. Did Jordi also say mean things to you?'

'I guess so.'

'So it sounds as if he's at fault too. Will it make you feel better if you say sorry again? And then do something nice for him? After that you have to take his word for it that everything's okay. You've forgiven him, he's forgiven you, now you need to forgive yourself.'

Willow was making Iris's brain stretch.

'Anything else?'

Iris faltered. There was the big thing.

'You don't have to.' Willow struggled to get out of the beanbag and failed. 'Let's put some music on instead.'

'There is something else! What would you do if your parents were doing something wrong and you knew about it, but you were too scared to talk to them about it?'

As soon as she'd spoken, Iris knew she'd made a big mistake. 'Never mind,' she said and stood up.

'Iris, my mom and dad are tax fugitives. Do you know what that means?'

Iris sat down again. 'Not really.'

Willow's blue eyes were bright against the thick rims of dark eyeliner she wore. 'It means my parents are greedy. They didn't want to pay the government money that they owed, so we moved here instead. We're in hiding and I doubt we'll ever go home. I'll have to go to college in Europe. So I understand exactly what you're talking about.'

'Will they go to prison?'

'They could. If someone turns them in. At first I figured that person was going to be me. But if I turned them in, where would that leave me? So, I settled for telling them what I thought about what they've done.'

'Oh.'

Iris ruminated for a few moments. *My parents aren't doing anything illegal, but things don't have to be a crime for them to be wrong, do they?*

'The important thing is that I've worked out how I want to act,' said Willow. 'Like, I've got principles for myself, you know? And that's separate from my parents' ideas about right and wrong. But it sucks to be in that situation, Iris. It really sucks.'

Jordi zoomed up behind Iris on his bike during her walk back to *Bosque de Nubes*.

'Where've you been?' she asked. Jordi wore a grass-stained sports uniform and had a pair of shoes slung around his neck.

'Football practice.' Jordi hopped off his bike and wheeled it. 'I am the best in the team.'

'You're so modest, too,' said Iris.

'Do you enjoy the ditch?'

It was true that Iris was walking in the ditch next to the road. She'd made a crown out of daisies to sit on her newly blue-tipped hair and was swinging a ziplock bag full of macarons that Shirley Dangercroft had forced on her. She climbed out so she could talk to Jordi better.

'I need to say I'm sorry, and I need you to be quiet now because I have something important to tell you.'

She sounded like a character on one of Elna's soap operas, but it didn't matter. Her life was a melodrama—and her parents were the villains.

Jordi miraculously kept quiet as Iris told him why her parents had sent her to Spain. He was silent when she told of her doubts about her mission, how deceitful she'd felt, and how she hadn't made friends with him for any other reason than that he was fun to spend time with. She listed all the ways in which he was a better friend than Violet. And he didn't blink once when she told him about recognising her dad's business logo on the brochure and had realised that she'd been lied to all along.

In fact, Jordi was quiet for so long that Iris started to panic.

'Say something, Jordi! Anything. Do you think I'm a terrible person?'

'No.' He didn't sound convincing and his brow was furrowed. 'Your parents should be setting better example.' And then, 'This is a big worry.'

'You're telling me.' Iris would have liked to say that she was going to stand up to her parents, make them change their minds, but she knew she couldn't promise that.

They walked together in silence for quite a while after that.

'I think my father and I should make plans to live somewhere else.' Jordi was morose. 'Maybe we can't stop this from happening.'

'I don't think the Dangercrofts will sell,' Iris said, remembering that Willow's family had nowhere else to go. 'And we know how Aunt Ursula feels about it. Maybe everything is going to be all right.'

But she didn't really believe that.

Jordi kicked the ground as he walked. 'Señorita Freer is going to die. I feel sad. Sad makes me hungry.' He stared pointedly at the bag in Iris's hand.

'Oh no, you don't want to go near these. Shirley Dangercroft made them. I should have thrown them away already.'

Jordi snatched the bag from Iris before she could stop him.

'Seriously, Jordi, they smell the same as crayons. Willow told me to never eat her mum's cooking.'

'Who is Willow?' Jordi spoke through macaron crumbs. He wasn't fazed by their lumpy consistency.

'She's the Dangercrofts' daughter. Oh! I almost forgot to tell you—I have another lead on the eyeball tree. Willow has seen it too. Well, she didn't realise what she was looking at, but she says she knows where it is.'

Iris pulled the regional map from her pocket. Willow had marked a rough location for the tree with a Sharpie.

'See? Aunt Ursula's land ends here, and here's the Dangercrofts' property. Willow said she saw the tree near here, same as your dad. Just a bit further south.'

Jordi was already on the last macaron. When he'd swallowed his last mouthful, he turned to her.

'You told this Willow *everything*?'

'No, of course not. I kept our secret. She wanted to see the painting that's named after me. We looked it up online.'

They'd reached the main gates, which Iris held open for Jordi to wheel his bike through. It had received a few new scratches during the Beast Car chase, but was otherwise fine.

'But maybe it's silly to keep looking for the tiger. There are other things to worry about,' she said.

'In 1589, a smuggling ship hit rocks off the coast near *Segur de Calafell*,' Jordi said cryptically. 'The ship was taking so much water and they were so far from land that the sailors decide to have a party instead of trying to save themself. So they drink all the rum and smoke all the opium instead.'

'I don't get it. You want to get drunk?'

Jordi scooted along on his bike. He had gained some of his usual pep.

'It means tonight we forget all these worries and go looking for the tiger.'

23

Iris set her alarm for midnight but couldn't sleep. She checked and double-checked the torch batteries, tucked the map and the catalogue into her backpack, along with a child's fur coat she'd found in the walk-in wardrobe (Beast Car Lure & Protective Decoy), a coil of rope, a water bottle and a compass that she had no idea how to use. There was no end of useful things to be found in the cabinets and drawers of *Bosque de Nubes*.

When she'd finished packing, her backpack weighed a ton or two. The minutes ticked over to twelve.

Out in the moonlit backyard, Iris felt as if she was in a clumsy dream. Jordi was going to leave his bedroom window open a crack. She circled Marcel and Jordi's cottage, trying not to step on any twigs that would snap.

There were two windows at the rear of the building. The window on the right had dinosaur decals stuck to the glass. It was ajar.

Iris tapped, softly at first, then louder. Eventually a tousled head appeared through the curtains.

'Why aren't you dressed yet?'

Jordi should have been ready to go, but he was still wearing pyjamas.

'I am sick.' He sounded like the Godfather from those movies that Iris's dad loved. 'I am doing nothing but vomit, and when I am not vomit, I am sitting on the toilet. Urghhh.'

He disappeared, and Iris pulled away from the window. When Jordi returned his forehead glistened with sweat. Even in the moonlight Iris saw his unhealthy pallor.

'Maybe I die tonight,' he said.

'It was Shirley Dangercroft's biscuits!' Iris finally twigged. 'I told you not to eat them, didn't I?'

Jordi rested his face against the windowframe and groaned. He could barely keep upright, let alone stand or walk.

'You can't come, can you?'

He shook his head.

'I won't go then, either. I can't go on my own.'

It was only a bit more than a kilometre to the supposed eyeball tree location, but it involved walking through dense forest.

'I could be better tomorrow?'

'Okay.'

Tomorrow was Saturday, and Iris was leaving on Sunday. Time was slipping away.

The tiger could be seen as just a small thing, but if she could figure out the puzzle of the painting, maybe she could be as brave as Iris Freer, who had risked her life on the battlefield. With bravery, maybe she could say something to her parents that could change their attitude to Aunt Ursula's estate.

Iris said goodnight to Jordi and pretended that she didn't mind that they weren't able to look for the eyeball tree.

The shadowhound waited for her on the steps, its lines clear even in the moonlight. It sat, nose alert to the air, and wagged its tail when it saw Iris. Iris tried not to look pleased. When she tried to get past, the dog moved to block her.

'I'll use the other steps then.'

But the shadowhound was waiting on these steps too. It nudged her away from the patio and bounded to the side of the house.

'I know what you're doing. You can't disappear for so long and then reappear and expect me to follow you.'

But Iris did follow, and the dog herded her to the front. The moon sat above the gardens, casting silver over the whole scene. The dog-shaped shadow crept up the driveway.

Iris pulled her coat around her tighter. The dog disappeared against a dark-green hedge. Iris studied her map. When she started to move, it trotted at her heels.

The path Iris needed to find was close to where she and Jordi had seen the Exquisite Corpse creature. She had to follow it into the forest until she found a low wall that divided the Dangercroft and Freer estates. The spot wasn't that far from the aqueduct, where they had already searched, based on Marcel's tip.

That's where the eyeball tree should be.

Iris walked along the raggedy edge where the forest started, clutching her torch. Underfoot, the grass crunched with the very beginnings of frost.

The path was narrow when she found it, but it quickly widened into a dirt road that ran straight and true through the trees.

'Dog, are we really doing this?'

The shadowhound nudged the back of her knees in reply.

Iris made her way up the tramped earth road with the shadowhound a faint breeze beside her. The trees were uniformly brown and eerie. The road was lined on both sides with the simplest of fences—just posts and coils of barbed wire.

'This isn't so bad, is it?'

Talking out loud to the shadowhound was mildly comforting. There was enough light from the moon, so

Iris switched off her torch. Clouds of mist hung near the ground.

Iris shivered. The temperature had dropped. She climbed a stile over the barbed-wire fence. After climbing, she turned to see if the shadowhound had managed the steps, but he had disappeared. The way they'd come was dark, except for the patches of mist spreading into the treetops.

More mist was coming; wet fingers that burrowed into the neck and sleeves of Iris's coat. It was now almost impossible to see so she turned on her torch again.

'Are you with me, boy?'

Iris whistled, hoping the dog would follow. The mist made a corridor. Iris steadied herself against a tree.

The path became visible again for a few metres. Iris turned a full circle to look for the shadowhound. It was a mistake—she lost her bearings and couldn't figure out which way lay forward. The mist swirled.

I'm alone, she thought. *Parents stuck me on a plane. Jordi stayed in bed. Shadowhound doesn't care. Aunt Ursula is never there.*

It was seriously tempting to close her eyes and rest, but instead Iris retrieved the compass from her backpack and tried to figure out how it worked. The needle spun nonsensically. She knew she had to keep walking or freeze to death; her jeans and coat were clammy with dew.

At the end of a long hill climb, Iris found herself above

the mist. Below was a layer of cloud, interrupted only by tree trunks bursting through. She walked down into another mist soup. There was the faintest whirr behind her, but when Iris looked, nothing there.

There was no way she could keep walking all night. Iris began to calculate: *If I find a sheltered place to rest, what are the chances that I won't freeze to death in my sleep? Or is it better to keep moving?*

Iris chose to keep moving, but was stopped again by a sound behind her. A low whirr, and an unfamiliar popping sound. She stood still until she placed it—it was the low purr of a car engine.

Iris turned. The Beast Car waited about fifty metres off. Mist rolled across its scratched duco and snarling grille mouth. Its headlights flashed, once, twice, a warning that it could charge at any moment.

Iris tried to play it cool. She started moving backwards until she was going as fast as she dared. The car followed her, with a constant rev. It stayed at a distance but it didn't let her escape.

Suddenly, Iris dived to the left, running through trees and ferns. She stepped into an unexpected hollow and jarred her ankle. Shrubs whipped her face.

The car lumbered after her, making up ground. Its big clawed feet travelled over the uneven terrain with ease. The next time Iris turned around, it was closer than ever and flashed its headlights again.

She stumbled to her knees, painfully, but she managed to pick herself up.

The mists had cleared and the pine trees had become more orderly, but there was no point running anymore. She would never be able to outrun it.

Iris's throat ached. Her shoes were sodden. She turned to face the car.

Its headlights were on; there were lights on inside the car too. All four doors swung open. The car sank onto its belly, claws tucked underneath. The silver bumper and grille sagged. The car quietened its revving to a purr, then turned the engine off completely.

Iris waited.

The car glowed yellow inside. One by one the doors slammed shut, leaving only one passenger door open.

Iris circled the car, keeping at a safe distance. The back seat was red velvet, the interior lined with cream silk and mahogany panels. As Iris moved closer she saw a moth-eaten cushion and a crocheted blanket on the seat.

When she was sure, she poked her head inside. The radio switched on and ragtime music filled the car. The lights flickered.

Using her last shred of courage, Iris climbed into the car and shut the door. It was warm inside and hot air seeped from vents. With the lights dimmed, and music playing softly, Iris curled into a ball.

When she woke, it was still dark outside. The car windows had fogged up. The lights were now off, and the Beast Car seemed to be snoring.

Iris tucked the torch under her armpit and aimed it at the catalogue of Uncle James's paintings.

She'd looked at the *Iris and the Tiger* painting so often she'd lost count. The eyeball tree was still there, and so were the waves and the wall and the window. Iris Freer stood with her hand on the windowsill, as she always did. She wore a two-tone stripy brown jumper and a determined look.

The catalogue fell into Iris's lap; she let her gaze soften. Maybe every time you looked at a painting it was new, because you looked at it through whatever mood you were in.

Iris Freer wore her frizzy blonde hair in two bunches that almost—if you weren't looking at them directly—looked like ears.

Iris sat up.

Wrong tiger, she realised. *I've been looking for the wrong tiger all along.*

The stripy brown jumper, the yellow hair standing up in two wild tufts.

Uncle James had painted each fold of his wife's blue skirt so carefully it was easy to miss what could be a stripy tail, cleverly camouflaged. Then again, it could have just been the way the skirt fell.

Iris had found the tiger.

She put her coat and shoes on, and stepped out of the car. The windscreen wipers fluttered when she shut the door. She stretched her arms over her head and her back cracked.

She was no longer in the pine plantation.

While Iris slept the Beast Car had rolled to a dark and ancient part of the woods. The trees arching above were so tall she couldn't see where they ended. It was like standing in a cathedral.

A breeze wove through the grove. There was a pale-blue glow in the distance.

As Iris walked, her feet threw up dust, and after a moment she could make out a faint voice.

Irissssssssssss.

The blue light grew until the grove was fully illuminated. A stand of trees emerged, from faded nothings to something that had always been there. Purple and blue trees as pretty as they were in the painting,

Irisssssssss.

Iris touched the smooth lavender bark. It was real, solid under her touch. The leaves were thick and rubbery, as big as her hand and inky in colour. Iris kept moving, looking for a wall, a window and an impossible sea.

She stepped around a tree and it blinked.

The eyeball tree.

An eye as big as a dinner plate nestled into its trunk.

The folds of bark were eyelids fringed with mossy lashes. It watched Iris pass.

Irissssssss.

At the centre of the trees was a bare patch of dirt where the wall, the window, the impossible sea and Iris Freer the tiger should have been.

Iris waited. Nothing happened.

It seemed the trees—the ancient ones and the newer blue-and-purple ones—were all holding their breath.

What could be wrong? Iris racked her brain.

She remembered Señor Garcia's trick at his special tree.

Iris found a stick and made a flat space in the dirt. She was no great artist, but she drew a woman's face, with a kind smile, curly hair and big eyes. Iris pictured the photo of Iris Freer and Aunt Ursula laughing, and did her best to draw the original Iris.

When she finished, she stepped back.

Did it work?

A blue brick appeared in the clearing. A second brick stacked on top, then several more came to form a line across the ground. The wall built itself out of thin air, and left a hole for the window.

Iris raised a hand to her hair; it felt lighter and fluffier than usual. When she stepped forward, she was struck with dizziness. Her legs were now long and thin—she was further from the ground than usual!

Irisssssss, sighed the voice happily.

The wall was complete and the sound of the ocean came from the window.

There was the faintest imprint of a hand on the dusty windowsill. Iris placed her hand over it, standing exactly where the other Iris had once stood.

It was daytime, clear and bright. The sea was still and endless. The wall went down further than Iris had expected, almost as if she was at the top of a tower and the sea was calm.

Aunt Ursula is wrong about what the water means, Iris realised. *The painting is about Iris Freer's feelings, not Uncle James's.*

A rough sea meant she hadn't been calm or happy. The tower could be a sign that she felt trapped. No one could know for sure why she'd felt that way—it could have been living so far from home, or because people didn't approve of her, or memories of the war.

But Iris finally understood. She'd found her own version of what the painting meant.

There was a commotion when Iris walked out of the forest, her hair and legs returned to normal. The entire household had gathered on the patio. Sunrise painted the rear wall of the house pink and orange.

'Oh, oh, I almost gave up atheism for you!'

Aunt Ursula rushed forward. She wrapped Iris in a hug and this time Iris did not resist.

'I knew you would return, I shouldn't have worried so. Jordi assured me you knew what you were doing.'

Jordi waved from a banana lounge. He still looked sickly green and wore a blanket as a cloak. Marcel and Elna were there too, dressed in coats and boots.

'I didn't know what I was doing at all.' Iris waved weakly. To her surprise Marcel smiled at her. Even Elna seemed relieved.

'Show me someone who does,' said Ursula. 'You're not going to like this, but I contacted your parents in a fit of guilt. Let's go inside and have a hot drink before we call them, shall we?'

24

After a hot chocolate, a plate of *churros* and a bath, Iris was ready for the phone call. She decided to open with a lie because, after all, her parents had told her plenty of those.

'It was all a mix-up,' she said, once her mum had stopped with the hysteria. 'I got up early and went for a walk. I left Aunt Ursula a note, but it must have blown off the table.'

Iris sat alone in the upstairs sitting room. Marcel had fixed the old dial telephone. From there she could see the grand piano. It had been over a week since she had witnessed the mutant ants and this whole thing had started.

'We're very relieved to hear you're safe,' said her dad. They had her on speakerphone.

'Are you?' asked Iris. 'Because it seems to me that the

most important thing is that I do exactly what you want me to do over here.'

'I don't think that's very fair.' Her mum's voice was tight. 'You're so far away and we have no idea what's been happening. Of course we're concerned.'

'I think it's very fair.' Iris's pulse raced but she had to say it now or she never would. 'And I can tell you what I've been doing. I rode a horse for the first time ever, and I ate blue soup, and I learnt about art and I tried to draw and I went to Barcelona, and I made new friends, and…I think that you're more worried about yourselves than me.'

'Everything we do is for you,' said her dad.

Iris ignored him. 'I didn't take your advice, by the way. I found out more about the people who are trying to buy *Bosque de Nubes.*'

The line went very quiet. There was only the sound of breathing on the other end.

'It was a big surprise,' she continued.

'It's not what it looks like,' said her dad. 'It's complicated. We wanted to tell you—'

'No, it's not complicated! You lied! You said you wanted to protect Aunt Ursula's house. But what you really want to do is knock everything to the ground for a stupid amusement park.'

'There's a lot of money involved,' Iris's mum chipped in. 'Your father has finally managed to get back in the good books with his family with this deal—'

'It's more than an amusement park. It's a whole new concept involving beautiful gardens and landscapes and art and hotels. It's more of an all-round tourist destination idea.' Her dad was already slipping into his architect mode.

'I don't want to hear it.' Iris decided to use one of her parent's own lines on them. 'I'm very disappointed in you. I thought you knew better.'

It was satisfying, and true. She hung up the phone.

The greenhouse studio door was wide open.

'Hello?' Iris called out.

She could hear music and talking as she stepped inside. The insides of the studio looked the same as ever, but the gilt-framed mirror that usually lay flat against the end wall had swung open.

'Aunt Ursula? Elna said you wanted to speak to me?'

'Up here!'

Iris pushed the mirror open further. It was hinged along the side like a door, and it concealed a narrow staircase.

'I don't believe it,' breathed Iris. Now she knew how Aunt Ursula had appeared in the locked studio when she'd been terrorised by the paint.

At the top was a small attic with a bank of sloping windows. Aunt Ursula stood at an easel, palette and brush in hand. Iris recalled the times she'd noticed movement and shadows in those very windows.

Iris entered with the feeling that she was finally seeing the full truth.

A flowery bedsheet hung from the rafters beyond Ursula. Señor Garcia sat on a nest of beaded cushions in full, undisguised insect mode, wearing a fringed leather vest and an embroidered headband. A gerbera poked out of his vest pocket and he held a guitar.

'I need your opinion, Iris,' said Aunt Ursula. 'This isn't working and I'm not sure why.'

All those times I searched for Aunt Ursula inside, she was here, painting!

Everything in the secret studio was simpler than the luxurious house.

The floor was bare, except for a faded Persian rug, and there was a sagging couch by the wall. The wooden beams of the ceiling lay above, while the attic was bathed in daylight. Canvases and supplies were stacked neatly in the corner.

'Don't be nervous!' Aunt Ursula slid off her reading glasses and beckoned. 'Reynaldo informed me that you've already seen him in his insect form. Come!'

Iris stood next to her great-aunt to see the painting better. A packing crate tipped on its end held tubes of paint, brushes, rags and a jar for cleaning brushes. Señor Garcia waved at Iris and chirped.

Iris still wasn't completely used to seeing his buggy black eyes. She couldn't wait to tell him how she'd used his trick to solve the mystery of her painting.

The portrait was only half finished but Iris recognised the style.

'The arms are very insecty,' she said after a moment. 'Maybe they should be more human, like, in their position? I don't know.' She flushed.

Señor Garcia clicked and waggled his head. The strap on the guitar kept slipping off his green shoulders.

'Good point. He says it's hard to look natural when he's never held a guitar before.' Aunt Ursula circled the easel. 'You're right, Iris. I'll do the arms again.'

'Aunt Ursula, how many of Uncle James's works did you actually paint?'

'Ahh. When Jordi told me that you'd visited the Dangercrofts for a second time, I knew you were onto me.'

Aunt Ursula put down her brush.

'I did a good job ageing Shirley's painting, didn't I? It's amazing what you can do with a bit of sand and varnish and a hairdryer. I used a compass point to pick cracks in the paint.'

She didn't seem at all ashamed about discussing her forgery techniques.

'My portraits of Reynaldo have been my private project for years. I found my muse in him. You only have to look at him to be inspired.'

They looked at Señor Garcia. He was deep in conversation with the gerbera in his buttonhole.

Iris pictured the number of zeros on the cheque written by Shirley Dangercroft.

'You didn't answer my question. People bought your paintings because they were supposed to be by Uncle James. Lots of people, not just Shirley Dangercroft.'

'*Bosque de Nubes* is a huge estate. It's expensive to run, Iris. It takes a lot to keep it from falling into ruin. I only wanted to keep its magic from being lost. And I needed money to do that.'

Iris was not in the mood for being lectured on practicalities and money again—not after the phone call with her parents.

'Do all adults lie so much?' she asked quietly.

'I would like to tell you, poppet, that adults do not lie, but I can't tell you that in good conscience. Sometimes I feel as if my entire life has been a lie.'

Aunt Ursula led Iris to the couch. Señor Garcia began stacking cushions and placing them in the corner.

'You look upset, Iris. Can you tell me what this is about?'

Iris swallowed. In a moment the tables would turn and it would be Aunt Ursula who was disappointed.

'My parents haven't been telling the truth, and maybe I haven't been either.'

Aunt Ursula nodded encouragingly.

'They sent me here to find out who might inherit *Bosque de Nubes* when you...in the future, that is. They were hoping that maybe I, or my family—'

'Oh, I knew that,' Ursula said, much to Iris's surprise. 'It was my first thought when your mother rang. After all those years, I knew something had to be up. She hardly had the greatest time when she visited. It's nothing to feel bad about. Your mother has always been—how shall I say?— practical. Let's go with that.'

Tears sprang up in Iris's eyes.

All this time, she thought, *Aunt Ursula knew. I didn't have to pretend.*

'There's more.' Iris forced herself to complete the picture. 'My dad's firm is part of the group trying to make the theme park happen. I found a brochure with his company logo on it.'

Ursula's mouth made a perfect O.

'If my parents get their hands on *Bosque de Nubes*, everything will be be lost. And it will be all my fault.'

Her tears fell, then multiplied into embarrassing sobs.

Señor Garcia stalked past the couch, trying to exit without a sound.

'Oh, you poor dear.' Ursula put her arm around Iris. 'If it makes you feel better, I've so many secrets I'm confused about which ones to keep, and which ones to tell.'

Iris wiped her nose. 'You have to tell my parents that you hate me, and that we didn't get along at all! And then you should say that you'll never, ever leave them anything in your will.'

My parents will think I'm a loser, she thought, *but that's better than helping them.*

Aunt Ursula made Iris look her in the eye. 'It's not your fault and I don't blame you. Leave it up to me. I've been through wars, remember? A few pesky businesspeople are hardly going to defeat me.'

The cottage was unlocked, so Iris let herself in.

Jordi lay on the couch, surrounded by comics and computer games and bottles of soft drink.

'I am starting to think about pizza,' he said when he saw Iris. 'I think this means I am not going to die. It's a pity. You were going to get my bike and my football.'

'That's a bummer.' Iris nodded towards the kitchen. 'Your dad's not home, is he?'

'You are safe.' Jordi wiggled up to a sitting position. 'You may not believe it, but he likes you. I think he is going to ask Señorita Freer to let you visit every year, so I learn more English.'

Iris sat in the armchair. She'd love it if she could come to Spain every year too, but there weren't going to be any more visits. Her parents would probably ground her for life. It sucked that Jordi and Willow lived in Spain.

'You didn't tell him that my dad is in cahoots with the developers, then?'

'I don't understand *cahoots*, but you are not your parents, *si*? You can't help the things they do. Anyway, I am going to make an internet petition against the park. My teacher has decided it can be the class project.'

Iris poured herself a glass of flat lemonade. 'I got my times and days mixed up. I fly tomorrow, but at 3am, which means I really leave tonight.'

Jordi looked crushed. 'Then you must tell me now. You were gone all night—what happened?'

'Well, I found the tiger. And it's nothing like what we thought it was.'

'I can't believe it!' Jordi hit his doona repeatedly. 'I'm a bummer.'

Iris put the catalogue in front of him, but he pushed it aside.

'I already see the painting—tell me about the tiger. Did it try to eat you?'

'Look,' Iris insisted. It was so obvious to her now that Iris Freer was the tiger, she couldn't *not* see Iris Freer as a tiger. 'Look again at her jumper and her hair and her skirt. Do you see it?'

'Just tell me about the tiger.'

Iris sighed. The fun of the painting was in seeing it for yourself.

'Then try this. What if she had a tail? Can you see if she has a tail? Anywhere?'

'No,' said Jordi. Then, 'Oh. Oh. I see it. A blue tail. Wait. Tiger stripes, ears, oh! Wait! She is the tiger!'

'Finally!'

'I am blind. Or an idiot, maybe.'

'Everyone is an idiot in that case. In all the art books I read, no one said who the tiger was. Even at the gallery—nothing.'

Iris felt bad that she hadn't told Jordi everything. But she wasn't sure that Señor Garcia's secret was hers to tell, or Aunt Ursula's either.

'I have a big question about all of this: if there was a battle between a tiger lady and an Exquisite Corpse creature, who would be the winner?'

Iris laughed. 'You really are feeling better, aren't you?'

'If the lady had mutant tiger powers, it would be a close fight.'

'You should introduce yourself to Willow Dangercroft and then she can draw you a comic about it.'

Jordi screwed up his face. 'You are okay, Iris. But I am really not sure about other girls.'

25

The book had a brown leather cover and cream pages inscribed with faded ink. It held the stories of a brother and sister who had painted together as if they were the same person. It had started when Aunt Ursula moved to Spain to live with James and his wife, Iris.

At first, James and Aunt Ursula had painted separately, sharing only the greenhouse studio and their paints. Everything changed, though, when Iris Freer died.

'James lived for her,' Aunt Ursula had said when she gave the book that recorded all their paintings to Iris. 'The only other thing that mattered to him was art. After Iris's death he stopped eating and talking and even painting. He never went outside, never smiled. I grew very scared.

'I knew I had to make him paint, and the only way I

could convince him was for us to paint together. It kept us both afloat, really.'

Iris stood alone in the ballroom and tried to match the paintings on the wall with the entries in the book. The paper was crinkled at the edges and smelt musty.

The book contained pages and pages of lists made over forty years. Each page was ruled into columns, with dates of when a painting was started and finished. James had started the book on his own and had finished it with Aunt Ursula. They'd used their initials to show who had done which stage of the painting, and there were spaces for the title, date it sold and price. The initials *J.F.* looked remarkably similar to *U.F.*

Iris searched for *Iris and the Tiger* first. Uncle James had painted it six months before Aunt Ursula had come to Spain permanently. She discovered that James had also painted *Courtly*, the tennis court painting, on his own, a few years before *Iris and the Tiger*.

Those flowers have been playing tennis for a long time, she thought.

Most other paintings on the ballroom wall were untitled, so Iris had to play a guessing game. There was a listing for *Ant Sonata*, which had to belong to the grand piano in the painting and the sitting room. James had mostly painted it, with Aunt Ursula adding the finishing touches.

Technicolour Storm might refer to a painting of a rainbow puddle, and then there was *My doctor told me*

I had a split personality. Iris thought that might belong to a painting of a man with two faces. It had been Aunt Ursula's idea—she'd made the sketches for it, and then she and James had taken turns to complete the painting.

Iris thumbed through the pages. There were no insect paintings on the lists, and no portraits of Aunt Ursula either. It made sense that the insect portraits weren't in the book, as Iris knew they'd been done after Uncle James's death. So Aunt Ursula must have done the portraits too, painting herself over and over and over, like some of the girls at school who were obsessed with selfies.

Something tickled the back of Iris's mind but refused to come into the light.

Aunt Ursula's face in the dark...

Iris left the ballroom and fetched her torch.

The east wing corridor was as dark as ever. Iris did not feel overjoyed to walk its length again, even though this time she was boss of her own feet. She was beginning to suspect the story about the rotten floorboards had been designed purely to keep her out, but she still jumped when the floor creaked.

The corridor went rapidly from merely dark to suffocating. Iris flicked the torch over the Aunt Ursula portraits hanging on the walls. There were so many of them.

The air grew colder as she passed the pale rectangles of doors to unknown rooms. Gradually, she was able to identify the shadowy shapes of half-moon tables and mini-chandelier lamps and a grandfather clock and the staircase leading up to the roof. She lost count at forty-seven self-portraits.

The corridor continued on, seemingly forever. The square of light behind Iris, the way to the normal house, was small and distant. Iris wasn't scared. She'd faced the famous cloud-mists, the Beast Car, the Exquisite Corpse creature, and the detested feet-boots.

Up close, the wallpaper was flocked with velvety fir trees. There were more canvases leaning against the wall, all of them with Aunt Ursula's face. The self-portraits had to number in the hundreds.

Aunt Ursula was a wonderful painter, easily as good as Uncle James. She hadn't hidden her too-big nose or her strong jaw. The self-portraits had their own luminosity: blush cheeks, sparkly eyes, smooth skin. A slender neck, dramatic bobbed hair. A young woman in the prime of life.

Iris recalled the photos on the sitting room walls, and how Aunt Ursula still looked almost the same as when her mum had visited thirty years ago.

She remembered standing in the forest at the painting place; what it had been like to have Iris Freer's pretty curls and long legs, even only for a few minutes. She pictured the way Señor Garcia's human shape rolled over his insect form.

Aunt Ursula had painted things as she'd wanted them to be. She'd said her whole life was a lie and then hadn't explained what she'd meant.

All these long years she's been cheating time itself by painting herself young.

Now Iris finally understood.

Iris dragged her suitcase down the sweeping carpeted staircase, hating afresh the detestable Chen Architects logo printed on the front. It was hard to believe that her ten days in Spain were ending.

Aunt Ursula had asked her to pack early so that they could go out to the forest together before the long drive to the airport.

She was halfway down the stairs when a painting spoke to her.

'Beware, Iris,' it said in a tinny voice. Iris stumbled— only her suitcase, with its sturdy handle, saved her.

The talking painting was very old, and showed a voluptuous young milkmaid lying on a chaise longue. She held out a hand-painted sign: *Iris Danger.*

Iris looked at the dried ridges and cracks in the paint; it was as if the sign had always been there.

'I'm Iris Chen-Taylor,' she told the milkmaid, 'not Iris Freer. So, thank you for your concern, but you don't need to worry.'

Iris sat on Aunt Ursula's canopied bed while her great-aunt sponged makeup onto Iris's face.

'Did you find what you were looking for in the forest?' Aunt Ursula asked.

'I got caught in the mists,' admitted Iris. 'That was scary. But beautiful. And I found the place where Uncle James painted *Iris and the Tiger*. Well, I suppose he didn't exactly paint it there, but I found where the painting is set.'

'We used to sketch outside and then take it to the studio.' The feathery strokes of the makeup sponge were relaxing against Iris's cheeks. 'No run-ins with the Exquisite Corpse creature?'

'No. I wonder where it's gone. I did see my friend, the shadowhound, though. That's what I call him, anyway.'

'Iris used to call him Mister Come-And-Go. She loved that dog.' Aunt Ursula stopped. 'I think I'm done. Tell me what you think.'

Iris rushed to the vanity table. Aunt Ursula had painted the apples of her cheeks golden yellow, blending into brown stripes on the sides of her face and forehead. Her nose was dark brown; she had whiskers, white eye sockets and a funny, square mouth. The blue ends Willow had put in her hair still looked good, even though her mum would probably make her cut them off as soon as she got home.

'It's perfect!' she said as Aunt Ursula washed her hands in the en suite. 'And you're sure it comes off easily?'

'Did I say *easily*?' Ursula returned to the main room.

'We can try with some cold cream. You might have to put up with looking a bit fancy for the plane trip home, though.'

She joined Iris at the mirror, bumping her along the seat. Aunt Ursula wore none of her usual gemstones on her fingers or neck. Instead she was dressed plainly in white. Iris gazed at her great-aunt's reflection. She'd plaited Aunt Ursula's thin hair with ribbons and flowers, mimicking the style of the Mexican lady with the monkeys.

I wonder how much older you'd look without the self-portraits? she thought. Aunt Ursula had looked so gaunt and drawn after their trip to Barcelona.

I suppose she can't leave here too often, or for too long. Señor Garcia too, unless he wants to be found out.

'You look pretty,' she said out loud.

'You're very kind. But I was never a great beauty, even when I was young,' Aunt Ursula replied. 'It never bothered me too much. Show us your teeth.'

Iris bared her teeth and Aunt Ursula laughed. 'There's a tiger, if I've ever seen one,' she said.

'Explain Day of the Dead again,' Iris said.

Señor Garcia had taken them out to the forest in a golf buggy that Iris suspected had been obtained by dodgy means.

'It was my favourite part of the year in Mexico. On All Soul's Day people go to the graves of their family members, and keep them company. They drink and eat and play music—a proper party. The living and dead come together for one night. And then they go their separate ways for another year.'

The trees were shadowy giants, streaked with the light from their hurricane lamps. Señor Garcia followed behind them, pushing a wheelbarrow along the uneven forest path.

Don't think too much about the living and dead hanging out together in the forest, Iris told herself.

When they reached the clearing, Iris had to pretend that she hadn't known James and Iris were buried on the estate. Aunt Ursula unpacked the wheelbarrow. Together they laid a picnic blanket between the two gravestones.

After dozens of candles were lit, the clearing was hazy. They piled the packets of Spanish lollies on James's grave, and croissants and a bottle of champagne on Iris Freer's. Aunt Ursula brushed the graves with a cleaning brush, while Iris unwrapped a basket of sugar skulls painted with food colouring. The flickering light cast ghoulish shadows across Aunt Ursula's face.

What would happen if she stopped painting herself? Iris thought. *Would she just age at a normal rate from that point, or would she immediately collapse in a dusty pile of bones and clothes?*

Painting yourself young seemed like the kind of thing a person couldn't do forever, but Iris didn't want this to be the only and last time she ever met her great-aunt.

When they'd finished tidying up both graves, Aunt Ursula draped them with chains of paper skeletons.

'Will people find any new insect paintings by Uncle James?' Iris asked.

'I hope not. I prefer to paint just for myself these days. After I found my own way with my painting, I realised that I didn't need to be a part of anyone's club to make art.'

Aunt Ursula appealed to the towering trees.

'But it took me too long to find my purpose in life, and now I don't want to stop.'

Iris took a deep breath. 'Aunt Ursula, I'm going to do everything I can to convince my parents to pull out of the theme park.'

Aunt Ursula smiled. 'Iris, my brother made himself sick with worry about *Bosque de Nubes* being destroyed or discovered, but it never happened. He made all our servants promise not to talk and they never did. We were always safe, even when the political situation here got rough. *Bosque de Nubes* has been very good at keeping its secrets, over the years. Anyway, I have a new plan.'

'What is it?'

'Something mysterious has happened here this week. The magic has been more active, as if it's been refreshed. Maybe *Bosque de Nubes* is a place that needs someone young and full of dreams. So I've decided to leave you the estate, young Iris. The whole kit and caboodle—house, land, all the paintings, everything.'

'What?' Iris wasn't sure she'd heard correctly. 'No! That's exactly what you shouldn't do! That's what my parents want.'

'But what if—' Aunt Ursula, dressed in white and topped with ribbons and flowers, seemed to pulse with energy. 'What if you didn't inherit the estate until you were eighteen? *What if* I can one hundred per cent guarantee that I will stay alive for another six years until you're of age? What about then?'

A normal person would argue, of course, that this was an impossible guarantee to give, but Iris knew it *was* possible.

It might even be possible for Aunt Ursula to live forever, she reminded herself. *You haven't ruled that out.*

'I do want to come back,' Iris said, at last.

Aunt Ursula beamed. 'Then it's settled,' she said.

Elna had turned on every light in the house, so that the windows spilled yellow across the front yard. The cream car was parked in front of the fountain and the sky was infinitely starry. Señor Garcia had already put Iris's suitcase and her purple backpack into the boot.

Aunt Ursula and Iris wore matching fur coats that they'd dragged out of the upstairs wardrobe. Iris felt elegant for the first time ever, even if her coat dragged on the ground and the tiger stripes hadn't washed completely off her face.

She took in a lungful of cold night air as if she was trying to breathe in Spain and keep it there. Now that the week was over, Iris began to wonder if she'd made the most of her visit to *Bosque de Nubes*.

She thought of her life in Australia. There were going to be some interesting conversations with her parents when she got home. And after making such good friends, so quickly—with Jordi and Willow, and even Elna—it was going to be difficult to return to school, and her shaky friendship with Violet.

But the world was bigger and more full of possibilities than it had been before, and Iris would never forget that. She'd hold on tight to everything she'd learnt at *Bosque de Nubes*.

'Are you ready?' Aunt Ursula asked.

Iris wasn't. Jordi had promised he would be here to see her off, but he hadn't shown. Maybe it was better that she was leaving at night. It would have pained her more if she could have seen the stables and the greenhouse and the cottage and the big mansion clearly.

'We'll be late if we don't leave now.' Aunt Ursula shepherded Iris into the back seat.

The car slid away from the house and along the driveway. Señor Garcia turned to check they'd put their seatbelts on and chirped loudly when he saw Iris kneeling on the seat to look through the rear window.

Jordi was running behind their car, a light bobbing up

and down with him. Iris rolled down her window and stuck her head out.

'I will email you!' he yelled. 'And video chat, promise?'

'Yes!' Iris waved until her hand felt like it was going to drop off.

Behind Jordi, beyond the edge of the road, she glimpsed something half hidden in the forest. The Exquisite Corpse creature ran alongside them, dodging trees, but keeping pace. Its eyes flashed like coins in the darkness; it was fleet of foot and free.

Acknowledgements

Iris and the Tiger has had a long gestation, and many helpful readers along the way.

The book started in a cabin in the forests of Oregon, where I drew, hiked, played, photographed, read and dreamt of surrealism. Many thanks to Caldera Arts for hosting me, and particular thanks to Elizabeth Quinn and Kathy Spezza for their support during my residency.

Heartfelt thanks to the friends and peers who read and gave thoughtful feedback on my many drafts: Andrew McDonald, Myke Bartlett, Chris Miles, Jack Nicholls, Gabrielle Williams and Marisa Pintado. Your diplomacy, encouragement and keen interest carried me through. Thanks also to Ed Moreno for his Spanish language skills.

Every author needs a good day job, and during the writing of this novel I've been lucky to be part of the Booked Out Speakers Agency, Readings and School of Life families.

Thanks to everyone at Text for their ongoing belief in me, and particular thanks to Rebecca Starford for her calm, organised and rigorous editing.

Finally, thank you to my family and to Grant, for being there for me in every possible way.